D1111957

"I want you to watch Serena," Thorn said

"Particularly when it comes to members of the opposite sex."

Polly stared at him incredulously. "You can't be serious?"

"Believe me, I've never been more serious," he went on. "I don't want Serena—looking around."

Polly felt a hate rising in her. But curiously, for all her anger, she stood magnetized as he ran his fingers sensuously through her hair. When his lips closed on hers, her own clung back.

"You're a very desirable woman," he said. "Your man in England must have been mad to let you go."

Polly pushed herself away from him. She shook her head as if to clear it. This was too preposterous. Did this arrogant man think he could reserve one woman, yet play with another?

OTHER
Harlequin Romances
by JOYCE DINGWELL

Many of these titles are available at your local bookseller.

For a free catalogue listing all available Harlequin Romances,
send your name and address to:

HARLEQUIN READER SERVICE,
M.P.O. Box 707, Niagara Falls, N.Y. 14302
Canadian address: Stratford, Ontario, Canada N5A 6W2

The Angry Man

by

JOYCE DINGWELL

Harlequin Books

TORONTO•LONDON•NEW YORK•AMSTERDAM
SYDNEY•HAMBURG•PARIS•STOCKHOLM

Original hardcover edition published in 1979
by Mills & Boon Limited

ISBN 0-373-02318-9

Harlequin edition published March 1980

Copyright © 1979 by Joyce Dingwell.
Philippine copyright 1979. Australian copyright 1979.

All rights reserved. Except for use in any review, the reproduction or utilization
of this work in whole or in part in any form by any electronic, mechanical or
other means, now known or hereafter invented, including xerography,
photocopying and recording, or in any information storage or retrieval system,
is forbidden without the permission of the publisher. All the characters in this
book have no existence outside the imagination of the author and have no
relation whatsoever to anyone bearing the same name or names. They are not
even distantly inspired by any individual known or unknown to the author, and
all the incidents are pure invention.

The Harlequin trademark, consisting of the word HARLEQUIN and the
portrayal of a Harlequin, is registered in the United States Patent Office and
the Canada Trade Marks Office.

Printed in U.S.A.

CHAPTER ONE

POLLY KENDALL walked down the wide stairs of the Hotel Southerly and out into the busy Sydney street.

For a moment, looking dispassionately at a city that was not her own city, she hesitated, sorely tempted to retrace her steps and join the party again. It had been a good party, with much laughter and happy singing, but when a farewell note had crept in, a farewell to *her*, she had known it was time to leave. Otherwise, she had thought numbly, I'll never go, and I must . . . I must.

She had risen from the table the returning staff had reserved for their breaking-up celebration, then waved a hopefully cheerful goodbye. Yes, she had agreed with the girls, she was the lucky one not to be going back as they were to a northern winter, then she had gone out quickly, wishing desperately that she *was*. Wishing she was returning to England—and to Steven. This winter, next winter, a lifetime of winters so long as there was Steven.

But there was not, not for her, not ever any more, so she was staying on in Australia—staying on, anyway, until it was safe to go back.

With an effort Polly stopped hesitating, straightened her shoulders, then began to walk.

She was pleased to see that in the time it had taken them to eat lunch the rather dull morning had improved to a bright afternoon. A good omen? She would hurry and find out.

She had left her shabby little secondhand car in the hotel parking lot, and her haste now had two more reasons other than the omen-searching. The first reason comprised the treacherous tears that were not far from falling so had to be hidden, the second the fact that she wanted to be on time to meet her new boss.

She reached the lot, found the car, opened up and started the engine.

Now she did allow the tears; tears were a therapy, it was said, and anyway, they would be dry by the time she reached Lime Tree, to which she had been summoned.

Slowly she released the brake. She cleared the parking lot, then set out, as directed, along the Great Western Road, and as she drove she wondered What? *What?*

What now? Polly thought. What is this new situation, and who is this new boss?

Her old boss had got her the position, but he had not been very informative.

'The firm's name is Clemance,' Mr Foxton had said rather vaguely, 'and it's an old-established one— grandfather, father, son, that kind of thing. The line is something in agricultural research as regards preventive medicine. The oldies are all passed on now, and it's Thorn Clemance, the university educated brother, who does the medical fact-finding. His junior brother Gil collects the specimens for him and later markets Thorn's advice to the big medical houses. But you'll be dealing with Thorn, the senior man.'

'You mean,' Polly had smiled, 'Thorn Clemance

will be dealing with me. It's usually a boss's prerogative, remember? But why? Why does he want *me*? I know nothing about medicinal plants.'—Nor about your particular class of statistics either, she could have added wryly, but I still came to Sydney with your team that's now going back again, but then it was Uncle Ben who manoeuvred that.

'Mr Clemance needed someone very urgently for Mrs Clemance,' Polly's old boss had explained, still vague.

'But I know nothing about nursing either!' Polly had concluded at once that this wife of Thorn Clemance was in need of some health assistance.

'Nursing is not required. Just youth, good company and immediate availability, were Thorn Clemance's words.'

'Oh, I'm available all right.' Polly had said it bitterly, but trying to keep the bitterness to herself.

'There you are then. What's wrong, Polly? Don't you want the job after all? You did ask me to——'

'Nothing's wrong, and I do want it.'

'Good then. I was beginning to think I did the wrong thing recommending you.'

'Did you recommend me?' Polly now remembered asking slyly. 'I was never your best figures girl.'

'But the best figure and the best looker. Both adding up to what young Mrs Clemance evidently wants. A contemporary, Thorn Clemance specifically told me—smart, mod—trendy, I think they say.'

'Also good company and available,' Polly recalled agreeing. 'Thank you very much.' She had not bothered to ask where the recommendation had taken place. Statistics of all kinds took heads of departments everywhere, and evidently one had taken her ex-boss to this place called Lime Tree, where she was now bound. Second turn-off, she had been briefed, after the last valley town but prior to the first Blue Mountains rise. She put her foot down.

There was little traffic at this time of day. In several hours the progress would be snail's pace, the Western Road, she had been told, put on a late afternoon snarl. But it was too early for that yet.

Had she not had other things on her mind, Polly could have taken the opportunity of looking around her as she drove, of enjoying the semi-rural scene in a leisurely fashion, but she did have other things, things that now and then blurred her eyes again, called for a quick brush of her sleeve over damp cheeks. Steven, she was thinking, I'm not coming back.

Because of this she did not see the small valley villages ... but she did see another village, a picturesque village not all that far from London; the little village that was home. She saw Uncle Ben sitting under the old apple tree that day, beckoning her to sit beside him. She heard him saying the things that he had.

'Polly girl, old, retired, unimportant busybody that I've now become, nevertheless I've successfully wangled you a job.'

'A what, Uncle Ben?' Polly had looked at him in amazement—and a little anxiety. Was the old pet having a turn? After all, he was getting on.

'A job. A post. A place of employment.'

'I have one already, Uncle, remember? On the village council.'

'Let me finish, Polly. I've wangled you a job away
from home.'

'I don't want a job away from home.'

'It's with a statistics team.'

'I don't know anything about statistics.'

'It's in Australia.'

'I'm not going to——'

'Where,' had come in Uncle Ben firmly and finally,
'you will remain for the next six months.'

Polly had stared at him, had disbelieved him, had
made him repeat himself, then stared at and disbelieved him all over again.

After that she had protested, declined, shamed, up-
braided him . . . but even as she had done so she had
sensed, as Uncle Ben must already have sensed, that
it might be an answer. Steven had drifted away from
her ever since her older sister Lucia had returned
from Canada to live again in the village. He had said
nothing about it, for the Stevens of this world don't.
Nor had Lucia, for the Lucias don't either. But the
evidence had been there.

It had taken Polly a long time to admit it. She had
known that Uncle Ben, in whose house the girls lived,
had known it at once, but stubbornly, jealously,
Polly had held on to a dream, held on to it as she had
held on to the simple friendship ring Steven once had
given her, even as she saw . . . but pretended not to
. . . two pairs of eyes meeting and merging across a
room, eyes that in their absorption noticed no one
else.

But for all Polly's unwilling awareness, that an-
nouncement of Uncle Ben's that day under the old
apple tree had shattered her.

'I can't go, Uncle Ben,' she had refused.

'You must.'

'Steven and I are engaged . . . well, sort of.'

'Sort of. Also not in your hearts.'

'I am in my heart,' she insisted.

'He's not in his.'

'He shouldn't have asked me if he didn't want to—want to——'

'*Did* he ask you, or did a star-struck girl make the first move?'

'If Lucia hadn't come back it would have been all right.'

'For you, Polly,' he said gently, 'but not for Steven. Look, little one, those two are made for each other, but because of their "niceness" it can't be. Not unless you take a hand.'

'You mean free Steven? Tell Lucia I made a mistake?'

'No, you'd only cry as you said it—I know you. No, I meant get right away, Polly, find someone else to love.'

'I won't. I couldn't find anyone.'

'You could try.'

'I could not!' she wailed.

'Polly, you're—how old? Nineteen. At nineteen a girl is a singer looking for a song.'

'I can't sing—you know that,' she pointed out.

'And you know I didn't mean it like that.'

'Then what did you mean?'

'I meant that Steven Marchant is not, and can't be, your song.'

'But he is . . . he always was . . . why, right from the beginning——'

Polly had thought back to that beginning. She had remembered their elderly neighbour dying, and some months later a man, a pleasant, blue-eyed, fair-haired man, looking over the hedge and saying: 'I'm the new owner. Aunt Phoebe left me Mulberry Cottage. I know nothing about mulberries or anything else in gardens, so will you please help? I'm Steven Marchant, and I'll be commuting to London. Now it's your turn.'

'I'm Polly Kendall. I live with Uncle Ben. I work in the village. I know very little about gardens either, but I'll help.'

It had gone on from there.

Oh, it had been good, it had been companionable, it had been wonderful. And now—and now——

'No, Uncle Ben,' Polly had refused.

'Yes, dear.'

'No! Don't ask me.'

'I have asked,' Uncle Ben had said firmly.

In the end Polly had agreed; too tired to fight stubborn old Uncle Ben any longer, she had taken the statistics job that he had found for her, and gone. Gone to Sydney, Australia. Gone for six months.

As the date for her return to England had come closer she had become excited. Evidently nothing had happened over there between her sister and Steven. Did that mean . . . could it mean . . .

Then Uncle Ben's letter had arrived asking for six more months . . . pleading for it . . . *demanding* . . .

'They're older than you are, Polly, older in their ways as well as their years. They move to a slower beat. They're more mature. They need more time, my girl.'

I won't, Polly had replied hotly, and the argument had started all over again, but this time by mail.

In the end she had agreed, but only if she could find more employment; the statistics team was going back, and jobs weren't so easy out here any more.

Almost at once her old boss had found her a place under a new boss ... had influential Uncle Ben had something to do with that as well? ... and now Polly was on the Great Western, going out to see a certain Thorn Clemance, who required someone young, good company and immediately available for Mrs Clemance. Young and available I am, Polly thought stonily, but good company after six empty months and facing six more empty months? Oh, no.

But her tears had stopped, anyway; they needed to for her to spot the small fingerpoint to Lime Tree. She took a sharp right bend, then proceeded along an empty, leafy country track until the road went no further. After that perforce she stopped and got out and looked around. It was very woodsy, she found, quite delightful. The only sound was crickets whirring, and ... listening intently ... some distant waterbells. Somewhere behind those stands of eucalyptus there must be a river of sorts. That was wonderful. She loved all kinds of water. River, stream, creek, it didn't matter, to Polly water was a solace, and she certainly needed such therapy now. She glanced at her watch, and decided to explore at once.

She left the car where it was, and set off, even though she knew she should have found the house first, probably set behind that tall peppercorn break on her left. But she was still a little emotionally disturbed, still thinking of the rest of the team going back to England, going with grumbles because of the season when she would readily have gone for a lifetime of bad seasons ... with Steven. She knew, too, that the river would help her, rivers always did. She would throw in some sticks, dabble her hands, unwind for a while. Catch her breath.

She pushed through the thick bracken, stepped carefully over delicate maiden fern and a few ground orchids, dodged a barrier of blackberry, then at last found the stream, and at once was rewarded. The course, by its very dark green quite a deep one, reflected in detail every passing cloud, each swaying leaf.

Polly glanced eagerly at her watch again. Still ten minutes to go for her appointment. She could, couldn't she? Within minutes she had pulled off her tights, tucked up the hem of her skirt. She found a convenient rock from where she could dangle her legs in the water to well above the knees, do it in comfort. She climbed out on the outcrop, then, for the first time in hours, she smiled, she relaxed.

In her new contented state of mind she did not hear the crackle of branches, the strong determined steps. Her first awareness of anyone else in her river paradise came with a distinctly intentional jerk upwards as she was pulled to her feet, then fairly heaved back on the grass behind the rock.

'You reckless little fool!' an angry voice shouted.

Polly had landed quite forcibly on the ground, and it took her a while to sit up without a reminding pain somewhere.

'You brute!' she shouted back at the man now confronting her.

'Sorry, but you had to be removed in a hurry,' he answered. 'There's a bait been set.'

'A what?'

'A bait.'

'To catch fish?'

'A very big fish. This one took a dog last week. He was doing what you were doing now—cooling off. He hasn't been seen since.'

'A shark?' she asked.

'Yes.'

'But this is only a stream.'

'A deep *saltwater* stream. There's not many sharks this far up, but one, for poor Rajah anyway, was enough.'

'It's horrible!' she shuddered.

He said soberly: 'I agree.'

He was looking at her very closely; Polly noticed the scrutiny, flushed and tugged down her hitched up skirt.

'You're Miss Kendall, aren't you?' he said. 'I saw your photograph.'

'You what?'

'I had to. I had to check you *were* young, promised good company, and——'

'And was available,' came in Polly thinly. She supposed Bill Foxton had shown him a shot of the statistics team, herself marked with an X. 'Yes, my name is Kendall. You would be a Mr Clemance.'

'Thorn Clemance.'

'The fact-finding, university-educated side of the two brothers.'

'I see you've been briefed,' he commented.

'Only sketchily. *Are* you the fact-finder?'

'Yes, you could say that,' he drawled back.

'Well' . . . Polly got pertly to her feet . . . 'What do you say to this fact, Mr Fact-Finder?' She gave a deliberately provocative bow as she presented herself to him, why, she could not have explained, she was reticent as a rule.

He looked her up and down, taking his time about it, and she felt that his narrowed green eyes missed nothing.

'Yes,' he said at last, 'you'll do, even though you're a reckless idiot, for after all Serena is something of an idiot herself. But don't let it happen again—that leg dunking, I mean. I have enough to do without dragging streams.'

'But what do you find apart from that?' Polly stubbornly persisted. 'Apart from my idiocy?'

'No finding. It's not necessary. You're needed for Serena, not for me.'

'Serena is Mrs Clemance?'

'Yes. She's waiting now to see you. When I noticed your car . . . not properly parked, incidentally . . . I guessed you'd come down here.'

'So you followed, believing prevention was better than cure?'

'There is no cure from a shark attack,' he answered tersely. 'When you put your gear on we'll get back.'

'Gear? I've only removed my shoes and pantyhose!'

'Still gear,' he shrugged, 'something Serena is very keen about. She'll expect the whole bit.'

'If you wanted someone well up in haute couture you should have gone elsewhere,' Polly snapped.

He shrugged again, saying almost uninterestedly : 'Put 'em on.'

Incensed, feeling a fool, hoping at least he would look away as she did so, Polly complied. It was not easy to wriggle discreetly into pantyhose, and she wished he would wander off. A tactful man would have. But he didn't, he stood there right to the final hitch.

After that, in silence, she followed him back to the road.

She saw at once that in spite of his haste to stop her meeting her fate in the river he had still stayed long enough to remove her car from where she had left it.

'No,' he corrected, evidently reading her thoughts, 'I told one of the men to do it.'

'Where is it?' she asked.

'Garaged.'

'That's kind of you, but seeing I only came out to be interviewed and will be leaving again——'

'Oh, no,' he corrected slangily, 'you're in.'

'In?'

'Accepted. In the employ. In which case you won't be leaving.'

'But I have nothing with me. No night things, I mean.' Polly flushed.

'Serena can fit you out. Heaven knows with the money she gets out of me she could outfit an army.'

'I presume you mean its female section,' Polly said coldly. Why did the man have to criticise his wife to her like this?

'Oh, she'd try the male section, too, after she'd done the girls. Clothes are very near to my Serena's heart. And that, incidentally, is something I want you to watch.'

'Clothes?' she asked.

'The male section.'

'I beg your pardon?'

'I particularly want you to watch Serena when it comes to members of your opposite sex,' he explained.

Again Polly said incredulously: 'I beg your pardon?'

'Although you are employed *for* Serena, you answer *to* me, and this is my cardinal requirement: I don't want Serena—well, looking around.'

Polly stared at him more incredulously than ever. 'You can't be serious!'

'Believe me, I've never been more serious in my life.'

'But surely you, as her—— I mean, surely you should tell her all that yourself.'

'Not when I pay someone else to,' he returned coolly.

There was silence for a few fuming moments from Polly. Then: 'I don't know if I want to be paid, if I want this job,' she said at last.

'But you want *a* job. Oh, yes, I was told that.'

'From Mr Foxton?'

'Yes.'

'Were—were you told anything else with it?' Polly always had suspected that Mr Foxton had been a confidant of Uncle Ben's.

'I think you mean about a man back in England. No. Yes.'

'What do you mean, Mr Clemance?'

'I was told nothing by your old boss,' he explained, 'but having a naturally suspicious nature I decided at once that if you desperately needed a job, it would be because of a man. It always is.'

'Please go on,' she said.

'I gathered, right or wrong, but it's right, isn't it? that you wanted a situation because you couldn't go back to where you came from. Not yet.'

'I can, but——'

'But you won't?'

Another silence from Polly, but this time not a dis-agreeing one.

'You're discerning,' she conceded stiffly.

'As I expect you will be with Serena. I meant what I said about the male sex. Here we are now.' They had reached the house, wide, rambling, single-level, spready, entirely surrounded with stone verandahs, an old colonial type of home.

Thorn Clemance tossed: 'You'll find her in the sun-room, that's it on the left.'

'But——'

'Yes, Miss Kendall?'

'Aren't you going to introduce me to your——'

'I've already wasted more time than I can afford. I'm a busy man. Just go in and bail her out of her fashion mags. She'll do the rest.'

Before Polly could answer him, he had turned on his heel and left. She watched him go; he was a very large person, broad-shouldered, muscular, not the ex-pected academic type. He walked angrily, if people can walk angrily, but then, looking back on their brief and rather stormy exchange, he seemed an angry kind of a man. She saw him cross to a large outer building, containing, she noted, a series of either offices or labs. Presently she heard a door slam.

She turned herself and proceeded to the verandah

room he had indicated. When her quiet knock was not answered, she knocked louder. When that was not answered, she turned the door handle and went in.

A girl lounged in a big banana chair, and she was so absorbed in one of the magazines that Thorn Clemance had contemptuously remarked upon to Polly that she did not look up even when Polly approached her.

It gave Polly time to stand—and to wonder at—Serena Clemance.

The wonder was because Thorn Clemance's wife, Polly decided, was the loveliest girl she had ever seen in her life.

Serena Clemance was misnamed. This, besides Serena's quite spectacular beauty, was Polly's first impression. Even in Serena's quiet absorption of the magazine, somehow the girl seemed unquiet. It was not just the moving mouth, the flicking lashes, the restless fingers, it was something in Serena. She was not serene, Polly decided . . . and she was not happy.

Her attraction was beyond argument, however. Deeply gold hair that must make her own colour a very plain tow, Polly thought, chiselled features that must emphasise Polly's own quite unprepossessing snub, a fair but coral-washed skin *without freckles*.

Admittedly there were imperfections. The lovely mouth pouted a little. The violet eyes, glimpsed behind the long flicking lashes, seemed somewhat bored. But these things could be rectified, and snubs and freckles could not. Polly sighed, then shrugged.

'Hullo,' she greeted aloud, 'I'm Polly Kendall, Mrs

Clemance. I just met your—I mean to say, I was just directed to come in.'

'Polly Kendall? Oh, you're the dear who's going to keep me company.' The pout and the boredom left Serena and she became entirely perfect.

'If I'll do,' Polly offered; already she felt she liked the rather sad-bright, very beautiful girl.

'Do? You'll be exactly what I want, Polly, what I must have. I was withering away here, with only a housekeeper for conversation.' Serena rolled her lovely violet eyes. 'Only Thorn.'

'. . . Only your husband!' But just in time Polly stopped herself from saying that.

'We can talk,' Serena Clemance was going on eagerly. 'Fashions, trends, plays, ballets—oh, it will be wonderful! Also you're English, aren't you?'

'Yes, but I left there six months ago.'

'I've never been there at all. I've never been anywhere. But now I will through you.'

'Don't expect too much,' Polly smiled. 'As you see, I'm no walking high fashion.'

'You are to me,' said Serena. 'Also, you don't talk only about digitalis.'

'What?'

'That's my dear Thorn. He has a one-track mind—agricultural research as regards preventive medicine,' Serena recited wickedly. 'Just now it's digitalis. Next month it will be——'

'He's the fact-finding agriculturist brother?' Polly knew it already, but she still said it conversationally —and curiously.

'Yes.'

'And the other Clemance brother? Gil, isn't it?'

'This will surprise you, Polly: I've never met him, for all our relationship.'

She was meaning, of course, her position of Gil Clemance's sister-in-law, Polly interpreted. Aloud Polly asked: 'You were married in Gil's absence, then?'

'Married? Yes—no—I forget.' Serena said it a little helplessly, and Polly, though unanswered, did not press the subject.

'Who else is there, Serena?' she asked instead.

'Mrs Ramsay, she's a widow, and she does the housekeeping. Then there's Ainsley, who does the books. Some helpers. But that's all. Now tell me everything, Polly. I see your hair is short. Is that the way now? And skirt lengths . . . long or not so long?' The girl's voice went on and on like a little stream, and Polly listened, amused.

She's so young, she thought, even though in actual years she's older than I am, yet compared to me she's still a rather naïve child. At times, and I suspect it already, quite a trying child, but one must try with children. Polly decided she would try with this one.

She smiled at Serena, answered every eager question, then presently found she was not being asked any more, and, looking across, she saw that the girl had gone to sleep.

She went quietly over and stood gazing at the lovely face a moment. It was not a happy face. She had felt that before, and now she felt it, but more strongly, again. There had been some kind of illness, she judged, or if not an actual illness then some period of strain. She gazed a while longer, then silently she withdrew.

She went into the passage, then followed a sound of domestic activity until she reached a large kitchen, its door wide open. She went in and introduced herself to the woman there.

'Mrs Ramsay?' she asked. 'I'm Polly Kendall.'

'Oh, so you've arrived then. Thank goodness for that! Now we might have some peace.' Mrs Ramsay tilted her head in the direction of the sun-room. 'Mrs Clemance has been worrying the soul case out of poor Thorn for you. At last he gave in. I'll make some coffee.'

'What about Serena?' Polly asked, thinking the girl might like to join them.

'Was she asleep?'

'Yes.'

'Then she'll sleep for an hour. White or black?'

'And what about Mr Clemance?' Polly asked next.

'He only comes in when his stomach demands it, Work comes first.'

'With his brother too?'

'You mean Gil?' Mrs Ramsay smiled indulgently. 'Oh, no, Gil would be here.'

'Gil Clemance collects the specimens, I believe?' Again Polly played the role of innocent.

'Yes. Right now he's in New Zealand and no doubt collecting some new girls as well as weeds. That's our Gil.' Another indulgent laugh.

'But Thorn Clemance stops at home?'—Well, why not, a married man would naturally do that.

'Yes, Thorn doesn't do field work. Madeira, dear, or fruit? And did Thorn show you your room?'

'No.'

'I expected that. As I said, work always comes first

with Thorn. When you're finished, I will. It's adjacent to Mrs Clemance's. Thorn probably knew how you young girls like to talk.'

'But——' Polly stopped herself just in time, as she had before with Serena. It was not her right to question the Clemances' sleeping arrangements, she decided.

'I myself don't live in, except when Thorn especially requests it,' went on Mrs Ramsay. 'I have an elderly father, and since his house is quite near it suits me to live there, unless asked. Not that Dad and I both couldn't live here at Lime Tree, it's certainly a big family place.'

Without a family, Polly thought. Aloud she said: 'Do you get asked?'

'You mean to live in? Oh, yes. Thorn's a proper stickler.' Without explaining that Mrs Ramsay added mischievously: 'Now his brother Gil——' and once more she laughed.

'Are you quite finished?' she enquired of Polly. 'Then I'll show you your room.' She got up busily.

Polly followed the housekeeper out to the hall again, then down a corridor to a very large, very sunny, self-contained bedroom with a bed already stocked with everything she would need tonight, nightgown, mules, wrap.

'I took them from Mrs Clemance's supply,' confided Mrs Ramsay. 'She has far too many.'

'I did intend to go back and get my own,' Polly attempted.

'No, Thorn said you would be stopping.'

'And what Thorn Clemance says is done?' Polly could not resist that.

'Of course.' Mrs Ramsay did not seem at all surprised, so Polly let it pass.

Her attention as she had entered her own room had been momentarily caught by the room to the right. It was similar to her own, but very untidy.

'Mrs Clemance's,' nodded Mrs Ramsay feelingly. 'I make it nice each morning, but five minutes after——'

'. . . Yes,' Polly agreed sympathetically, but her response was automatic. The untidiness had not surprised her, an unserene girl like Serena presumably would be untidy. But the singleness of the room, even though she had established this fact before, did surprise . . . and bemuse . . . her. A single room with a golden-haired, violet-eyed, beautiful wife like Serena seemed unbelievable.—A single room with a strong, hard, vital, undoubtedly sensual male like Thorn Clemance *was* unbelievable.

Concealing a doubt, Polly smiled pleasantly at Mrs Ramsay, assured the housekeeper that everything was perfect, then told her she would settle in. When the woman had left, she thought how silly she had been saying that; she had nothing here to settle, all her things were still in her Sydney flat. She must see to that tomorrow, that is if she still agreed to stay on. Yet what else could she do? No other job seemed to be offering, and for survival's sake . . . and Lucia's and Steven's . . . she had to remain. She was angry about the job, though, irritated by the housekeeper's 'Of course' when she had suggested that what Thorn Clemance said was duly done. What an autocrat the man seemed, what an arrogant, roughriding, self-satisfied cock of the walk! Already he had decided her future for her. 'You're in,' he had said. 'You won't be leaving.' She had rankled, but she had complied. Even needing this job, why had she done such a servile thing? Polly bit her lip.

But her crossness left her when Serena, awake again, came sauntering along the passage. She bore more armfuls of lingerie for Polly, beautiful flimsy things that Polly had never before worn in her life.

'But I've more than enough already, Serena,' she protested.

'So have I,' Serena laughed impishly. 'Thorn says the next lot I buy will have to go back.'

... And what Thorn Clemance says is done. Polly almost said it aloud again.

'Thorn's very kind,' Serena went on. 'He can look fierce, but he's not, not to me, just—just restrictive.'

'Restrictive?' queried Polly.

'At times he can be quite old-fashioned, very rice pudding. Did you say that at school about some of your teachers?'

'Yes, but I'd hardly think of Mr Clemance as rice pudding.'

'You'd think of him as rice with curry, then?' Serena became the imp again. 'A very hot, very strong curry—yes, that would be my Thorn.'

'Serena!' Polly felt that at least she should protest that.

'Oh, I really do love him, but at times——' A sigh.

... You are meaning times of single rooms. The thought flashed unbidden into Polly's mind. She did not know why she was preoccupied with that fact of rooms instead of a room, but she still was. It just didn't fit in with a man like Thorn Clemance.

'Serena,' she asked gently, carefully, 'have you been ill, dear?'

'Yes—no—oh, I forget. Please, Polly, don't let's talk about it. Let's talk about—about tomorrow. Yes, tomorrow.'

'No, not tomorrow, Serena. I'll be away then. I'm going into Sydney to close my city flat.'

'Then I'll come with you.'

'If your—if Mr Clemance agrees.'

'He will,' pouted Serena. 'He must.' She tucked her arm into Polly's and said: 'Come outside now and I'll show you around.'

Serena never got there, however. From the hall Mrs Ramsay called: 'The phone for you, Mrs Clemance, that dressmaker you were ringing yesterday.'

'Oh!' beamed Serena, immediately transported. 'Sorry, Polly, you go ahead and I'll catch you up.' Her voice, high and enthusiastic, at once began an excited recital to someone at the other end of the wire, and, smiling, Polly went out, knowing Serena would not catch her up, would immediately forget.

She went out to yet another long stone verandah.

It was a grand old house, she decided, a house fairly itching for a family. Was that the reason the Clemances had spread themselves? To make the house seem less empty? Resolutely Polly made a firm resolve not to think about that any more, but to accept things as they presented themselves, and the first thing that did present itself as she descended some shallow steps and walked along a garden path was a machine shop ... that's what Uncle Ben had called his handy corner ... and nostalgically Polly went in. She had always loved Ben's den.

She loved this den, too, loved the rough male atmosphere of it, the carefully-tended tools. She stood looking at the sledge-hammers, crowbars, crosscut saws, scythes and sickles, and all at once she was home again. She was helping Uncle Ben tidy up, and Steven ... Steven before Lucia had come back ... was joining them. He was smiling that open, blue-eyed smile of his ... (no narrowed, estimating green glint as in Thorn Clemance's glance) ... and suddenly, wonderfully, Cloud Nine was fitting its colours in the dark machine shop, and in Polly Kendall's heart. Oh, damn it, she was crying now.

'Look, young lady, if honest old leather, sawdust, creosote and fertiliser smells do that to your delicate senses, why don't you get out?'

The same as by the stream, Thorn Clemance had taken Polly by surprise. Not wanting to talk to him, to let him see that her tears were genuine and not what he thought, Polly leapt eagerly at the excuse he had offered her, and back away.

'Yes, they do,' she agreed. 'I must have some sort of allergy.'

'Then why did you go in?' Thorn Clemance had followed Polly out.

'I was just looking around. Serena started to show me, but——'

'But the phone rang and haute couture took over. Come and I'll show you myself.'

He strode ahead, and Polly had to run to keep up.

He made first for the gardens and glasshouses, nodding for her to follow. Some of the local crops, like foxglove, balsam and peppermint, were growing in open beds, but the introduced specimens were in carefully controlled shelters, and Thorn Clemance even re-checked the temperature after they had entered.

'What is it all about?' Polly asked as he came back to her side again.

'Health, in one word. In some of these earthy offerings could be an answer that manufactured drugs and scientific antibiotics have never found yet.'

'Has there been an instance?'

'Several.' His face had lit up, and his green eyes had widened, giving him a more boyish look.

'You love it, don't you?' Polly said impulsively.

'It was once my entire world.'

'Once?' The word was out before Polly could stop it. Annoyed with herself, she closed her lips firmly. Serena. But if marriage had changed the whole of his life, why——

Why were there two rooms?

She became sharply aware that he was gazing keenly, almost boringly, at her now, using once more that narrowed, enigmatical, estimating green-eyed glance of his. She took a tighter control of herself.

They reached one of a row of labs, and he opened the door.

'You peer through microscopes and magnifying glasses and make bubbly noises in retorts and then come to conclusions?' Polly asked flippantly, her mind elsewhere.

He responded drily: 'Something like that.' He conducted her out again and shut the door.

'There's more for you to see, but I'll have Ainsley attend to that.'

'Oh, yes, Serena mentioned Ainsley.'

'Ainsley isn't just my Girl Friday, she's my every

day of the week. We couldn't function without her. But she'll have left by now.' He was looking at his watch. 'She lives away from Lime Tree, which incidentally is a district as well as a house.'

'But not a village?'

'Our nearest village is Apple Tree, several kilometres away. One post office, one general store, and lately one doctor, I believe. But no great hardship, we're only some forty miles from Sydney.'

'I'm glad you mentioned Sydney,' Polly broke in. 'Tomorrow I would like to collect my clothes.'

'By all means,' he agreed.

'And take Serena.'

'No!' Thorn said at once.

'But I spoke about it to her, and she wants to come.'

'You shouldn't have spoken, and she can't.'

'But, Mr Clemance——'

'I said No. Incidentally, you can call me Thorn. Everyone else does, and it would be ridiculous you using a formal Mister. I'll call you Polly.'

'Very well.' Polly's voice was as bland as his had been. She paused. 'We were talking about Serena.'

'Who must be off the phone by now. It's nearly dark. Mrs Ramsay will have left.'

'Meaning I'd better get back to the house and prepare a meal?'

'By no means. You were not employed for that. Your only chore will be to drop the dishes into the machine afterwards. Oh—and play mother.'

'Play mother? But surely your—surely Serena does that?'

'When it occurs to her. Things don't always occur.'

'I see.' Polly was silent a moment. 'Is Serena—I mean, has she been——'

'Ill?' He beat her to it. 'No. Not in the way you may think.' He began walking to the house, the subject patently closed, and, the same as before, Polly had to run to catch up to him.

'But she still can't come with me tomorrow?' she persisted.

He stopped abruptly, so abruptly that Polly had no time to stop herself, and she stumbled into him.

He steadied her at once with a large hand on the thin silk of her blouse. He left the hand there until she caught her breath, and she could feel the heat of it through the fine material. One finger, the long forefinger, was just over her breast. She could feel the increased beat of her heart, and she knew he must feel it, too, through that long forefinger.

'I said she couldn't go,' he said in answer to her repeated question. 'And now' . . . removing his hand . . . 'we'll go to the house.'

He went ahead, switching on lights that Serena had not bothered about, turning on the television, a radio for music for them to eat to.

A steaming casserole was set out ready, an apple pie waited. Everything was prepared.

The meal went off pleasantly enough, Serena filling in any awkward gaps with her chatter. Fortunately she seemed to have forgotten about tomorrow.

After the meal, Thorn Clemance showed her how to stack the dishes into the machine, then switch on.

He retired to his study, and the two girls decided on records instead of movies and spent the evening selecting their favourites.

Around ten Polly found herself nodding. After all, it had been a long day, she thought, deciding on bed. She persuaded Serena to have an early night, too, and even coaxed her to a glass of hot milk, and had one herself.

'Because,' she smiled, 'I always find it hard to settle the first night in a new bed, and I fear your glamorous offerings are going to keep me awake.'

'Awaiting your Prince Charming?' Thorn Clemance had come in, but his nightcap was a whisky and soda. He held it in his large brown hand, the hand, Polly remembered, that he had put over her breast.

Polly was to mull over that 'Prince Charming' later in the evening.

In spite of her doubts about sleeping, she drifted off as soon as she went to bed.

She did not know what wakened her. A stir somewhere? A little night wind ruffling the curtains?— A soft step?

She opened her eyes and listened. She heard nothing. But she did see the quick flash of a torch. It came from the room to the right, from Serena's room. Then it flashed off again.

In spite of her curiosity, Polly drifted into sleep once more. She did not know how long afterwards she woke a second time, whether it was within minutes ... or hours. But she did know that steps were receding along the passage again, and from the direction of Serena's room. Of that there was no doubt.

Polly permitted a little thinned smile in the darkness of her own room. So Mr Thorn Clemance wasn't quite the cool, self-satisfied person he went to such pains to convey to people ... and to her. He was the same as other men, the same emotions, the same urges, the same demanding instincts as she had dreamed ... *and yearned for* ... in Steven.

Oh, Steven, Polly cried into her pillow, oh, Steven!

CHAPTER TWO

In the morning Polly was in full control of herself
again, and had she been truthful she would have admitted that she was beginning rather to enjoy the
situation. It was very satisfactory, she smiled secretly,
to find that the angry Thorn Clemance was not what
he put himself out to be, that for all his show of
arrogant sufficiency he was still insufficient ... still
the dependent male.

Why did he play-act, then? Polly asked herself.
Why the secrecy of last night? Why—two rooms?
For it always seemed to come back to that, she mused,
to two rooms.

'You look a trifle drawn,' Thorn Clemance com-
mented over breakfast on one of the stone verandahs,
Mrs Ramsay busy in her kitchen, Serena still in bed.
'Didn't you sleep?'

'I never do in a strange bed.'

'... Or when you lie thinking?' he suggested slyly.

'Thinking?' she queried.

'Whatever it is young women think of,' he
shrugged.

'I didn't lie thinking,' Polly said, 'and no doubt I
did sleep now and then. But' ... with sudden daring
... 'at one period I did wake.'

'Yes?' He was looking at her with apparent unin-
terest ... but somewhere, and Polly recognised it,
there was a demand there as well.

'There was a light last night,' she said boldly.

'Oh, come, you can do better than that.' His voice was deliberately taunting.

'It was in Serena's room.'

'Perhaps she couldn't sleep either and decided to read.'

'It was a flashlight,' said Polly.

'Now you intrigue me. What did you decide it was?'

'I decided it was your flash, Mr Clemance, unless there was someone else in the house.'

'There was not—and Thorn, remember, not Mr Clemance.'

'Thorn,' Polly said obediently.

'But you were right,' he drawled, 'regarding the flash. I was checking on Mrs Clemance. Any more questions?'

'Of course not. It's none of my business.'

'None at all.' A pause. 'But it is *my* business when I rouse a young woman from her slumber with my carelessness.'

'I never said so,' she protested.

'That's tactful of you, but untrue. You saw a flash, reached a natural conclusion, then spent the rest of the lone night——?' He raised his brows and smiled derisively across at her.

Polly caught a quick breath in disbelief. 'You're abominable!' she said angrily.

'Yet didn't you?'

Now Polly moistened her dry lips, searched for but found no words.

He let her silence continue for a while. He appeared even bored. But he was only being deceptive, because,

pouring coffee, then handing her a cup, he asked:
'And why not?'

'Why not?' she queried.

'Why shouldn't you dream? Why shouldn't I do
what obviously you had decided I did?'

'I don't understand you.'

'You understand perfectly,' he retorted.

Again Polly could summon no words.

She knew she had started the topic, but that didn't
excuse him for carrying it on so preposterously. He
was impossible, and she was glad when Mrs Ramsay
came in, and Thorn rose and declared that work
called. He advised Polly to seek out Ainsley, who
would finish any showing around he had neglected to
do last night. After that she could take off to Sydney
and collect her belongings.

'*But Serena remains here,*' were his final words.

'Yes, sir,' Polly could not stop that.

He shot her one of his narrowed green looks, then
left.

Mrs Ramsay, when asked, refused any help from
Polly, adding a succinct remark that once one person
helped another might, and she certainly did not want
Mrs Clemance in her kitchen. She said it fearfully, and
respecting her wishes, Polly went across to the col-
lection of labs and offices, and found the room she
sought at the end of the row. She knocked and entered, and a brown-haired girl sitting at a desk, a girl
with gentle eyes and a quiet, intelligent face, glanced
up and smiled at her.

'Ainsley?' Polly asked.

'Yes, and you're Polly. Welcome, Polly. Now sit
down and ask me any questions you didn't ask Thorn

—yes, he told me about you. After that I'll show you around.'

'I've been around. Mr Clemance ... Thorn took me. I've also explored a little myself. Only a little, but too far, I'm afraid. I found a stream and paddled my feet,' Polly looked rueful.

'I think I can guess what happened,' nodded Ainsley. 'Thorn can live up to his name. But in this instance you must forgive him. He lost a dog there last week. Since then the stream has been strictly taboo for both bathing and paddling. However' ... a warm smile ... 'how were you to know?'

'I expect I should have reported to the big boss and been briefed first,' admitted Polly. 'As it was the river called me before work did.'

'Rivers do,' agreed Ainsley. 'But all's well now?'

'With me, yes, but Mr Clemance——'

'Thorn is all bark.' Ainsley laughed at her words. 'Seriously, though, he's going through a very touchy time just now. Make allowances.' But she did not elaborate on that.

'You know the Clemances well?' Polly asked.

'Fairly well.'

'There's another brother, I believe.'

'Gil. Gil does the collecting and the marketing.' This had been said before to Polly, but not in that tone of voice. She looked across at the girl and the soft brown eyes looked frankly back at her.

'You would be pretty, wouldn't you, Polly?' Ainsley said ruefully.

'What do you mean?'

'So many pretty girls and only one plain.'

'If you're meaning yourself——'

'I am, and I am—plain, I mean.'

'No, Ainsley, I think you're——'

'Kind, intelligent, sympathetic—oh, yes, I know all that. But where does that put me in company like yours or Serena's?'

'But Serena is entirely different.'

'You mean she's beautiful? Yes, she is.'

Polly had not meant that, she had meant that Serena was married already, so obviously not in any market for any man—or Gil, for Gil, Polly felt sure, they were both talking about.

She even dared to ask it. She felt one could ask things of Ainsley. She said tentatively: 'Is it Gil?'

'Yes, Polly. It's been like that with me right from the first day I came here. It's steadily got worse.'

'Worse?' Polly queried.

'That's the wrong word, isn't it?' Ainsley gave a crooked smile. 'Look, Polly, shall we drop it? Now that you know my hopeless secret shall we let it rest?'

'If you wish.'

'I don't wish, but I accept the inevitable.'

'The inevitable?' asked Polly.

'Of knowing someone like Gil and being aware that it must finish at only knowing.'

'Must it?'

'With Gil's charm!'

'You have charm.'

'Not Gil's. Oh, you'll understand when you see him.'

'When will that be, Ainsley?'

'Quite soon. He should be back by the end of the month.'

'I gathered from Serena that she hadn't met him,

either,' said Polly. 'Does that mean that she and Mr Clemance were——'

'Thorn didn't bring Serena to Lime Tree until after Gil had left on his New Zealand stint, which turned out quite a long one,' answered Ainsley. If there was a sigh for her future with Gil in the explanation she hid it well.

'What are you doing with yourself today, Polly?' she asked.

'I'm collecting my things from my Sydney flat. Thorn has forbidden me to take Serena.'

'Yes, that would be best.'

'But——' Polly stopped herself. She did not want to learn once more that what Thorn Clemance said was done; it was becoming a little wearying. She rose from the chair and crossed to the door.

'It was nice meeting you, Ainsley. No doubt we'll be seeing a lot of each other. No need to show me around any further. Thorn managed to show me quite a lot last night, and I'll discover the rest as I go along. Anyway, you look as though you have your share of work.'

'More than a share. Apart from supplying a very real medical service, the Clemance brothers are certainly prospering. Yes, Polly, I'm busy. But thank you for calling in.'

She smiled, Polly smiled back, then went out to find her car.

It was garaged in another building along with several utilities and a tabletop. There was also a cream Mercedes and a rakish red sports—Gil's, Polly supposed.

She backed the car, then returned to the house to

tell Mrs Ramsay and Serena that she was going. Serena would probably pout, she had so wanted to come. On the other hand she might have already forgotten.

She found Mrs Ramsay, but there was no sign of Serena. Well, she didn't have time to look for her, the way she had worked things out if she left at once she could be there and back again in several hours. She supposed that at least she owed that to her boss.

She went out to the drive, got in her small car, then set off.

This time she looked around her as she covered the several miles to the Great Western Road. She found the situation quite charming, fields that could almost have been English meadows with their shining buttercups and their soft green grass hemming the earth track, everything soft and lush. She supposed it was the proximity to the cool mountains, now leaning in cobalt idleness against the western sky, that made the scene more like home than the other barer backgrounds she had been shown, and she smiled and for a few moments forgot her nostalgia.

But only briefly. In minutes Polly was regretting Australia as she never had regretted it before, though to do Serena justice the girl did have the sense to emerge from under the rug in the back seat *before* the Western Road and all its hazards could take over.

Hair prettily tousled from the roughness of the travelling rug, a little out of breath because, as Serena later complained, she had been stifled to death down there, she sat up triumphantly, exclaiming to Polly at the same time : 'See, I didn't forget!'

Polly looked at her first in the rear vision mirror and then over her shoulder. 'No, Serena,' she sighed, 'you certainly didn't forget.' She stopped the car and opened her passenger door. 'Come on,' she nodded, 'and I'll drive you back.'

Serena stared at her a long, pitiful moment, and then began to cry.

'Oh, darling,' Polly exclaimed, distressed, 'don't you see I *have* to take you back. He ... your ... Thorn said you were not to come with me. Serena, do understand.'

But even as she reasoned with her, Polly felt fury building up in her against Thorn Clemance. Even this early in their employer-employee relationship it was apparent to her that the man was stifling his young wife, caging her, and surely an intelligent person such as he must be should know, however worth the intent, that things can't be done like that.

As though she had spoken the words aloud, Serena began sobbing out her thoughts.

'Thorn never stops watching me, guarding me, restricting me,' she cried. 'He—he "dusts" me, Polly. He ties me up.'

'You exaggerate, Serena.'

'No!'

'He only does it because he loves you, dear,' Polly soothed.

At that Serena said a strange thing. She answered quite clearly: 'Oh, no, you're quite wrong, it's because he doesn't want *me* to love.'

'Serena, you're not making sense.'—And yet Serena's voice had been very lucid, very sure.

'But it's true, it's true. Polly, do let me come.'

Polly did not answer.

'He—Thorn needn't know,' Serena persisted. 'He won't go looking for me—he never does. He puts his nose in his lab, and that's that.'

'Serena, it would be dishonest.'

'He wouldn't know, I tell you.'

'Mrs Ramsay——' began Polly.

'She never bothers me, I don't think she likes me very much.'

'Thorn would find out. Men like him do.'

'Very well then, go on your way, Polly, but let me out first, and I'll—I'll run down to the river and throw myself in.'

'Serena!' Polly protested.

'I will, I will, I tell you. Polly, let me come.'

Polly hesitated. She did not like taking the car back to Lime Tree, for once there she could not trust Serena to stay by her side, the girl might well do what she had threatened. It would mean, too, she would have to alert Thorn Clemance at once, tell him all about it. She gnawed at her lip as she anticipated his cold face, his narrowed green look.

Serena was watching her. At the right moment she said simply and winningly: 'Take me, Polly—I'll be good.'

One more moment of hesitation, then Polly capitulated.

'All right then, you—you horror!'

Serena laughed, all sunshine again. She climbed in the front seat, and Polly released the brake.

The girl beside her behaved perfectly. She took a deep interest in the scenes around her, so much so that Polly asked curiously at last: 'You act as though everything is new to you, Serena, and it isn't, of course.'

For a moment a shadow came over Serena. She said in a low voice: 'I seldom went out—he never took me.'

Polly, after some consideration, decided not to follow that subject, and she talked of other things until she reached her small flat.

Serena was enchanted with the bachelor girl unit.

'It's pretty and snug. Ours was too big and too cold.'

'You mean yours and—you mean you lived in an apartment before you lived at Lime Tree, Serena?'

'Not one like this,' was all Serena answered.

She helped Polly pack her clothes, proving so useful in her skilled folding of them . . . she had a definite feeling for garments . . . that Polly felt mean merely returning her to Lime Tree after it was all done.

She could not take her into any of the big stores, though, it might prove hard to coax her out again, but surely a cup of coffee . . .

Oh, yes, Serena beamed, coffee would be fun.

Polly chose a hotel coffee shop she had often patronised, one with a decor that she knew would delight Serena. The girls walked round there together.

They were on their second cup, and Serena was deciding between an éclair and a macaroon to accompany hers, when the man stopped at their alcove.

'Of all this city's lovely faces, *yours*, Renie!' He was looking at Serena and there was bold admiration in his shifty eyes.

Serena, who had taken scant notice of him when he had paused at the table, visibly froze at that 'Renie'. She let the cake fork she held in her hand clatter to the floor, and when Polly got up again after retrieving it she saw that Serena was staring up at the man who had addressed her. She seemed made of ice.

Apparently not noticing her reaction, the man was saying: 'You shouldn't have dropped out like you did, Renie. Oh, I know you weren't ever around much, he saw to that, didn't he? but we all, us men, anway' ... a meaning laugh ... 'knew you were there. And why not now, darling? Beauty like yours shouldn't be hidden, Renie.—Or did someone hide it for you?' He came a step nearer.

'Anyway, the past is all history now, isn't it? A page turned and all that. But you should do some serious thinking, Renie, and *emerge*. After all' ... with cunning ... 'you wouldn't be financially pressed, eh?' He flashed what Polly personally found an objectionable smirk.

Serena must have found it objectionable, too. For the first time she took her fascinated gaze off the man and turned piteously to Polly for help.

'I think,' said Polly clearly, 'you'd better go.'

'But——' The man now turned to her, and his slackish mouth drooped even more. 'Look, who do you think you are?' he asked coarsely. 'Renie and I are old friends, we've known each other for years.'

'Well, obviously she doesn't know nor want to know you now. Go away, please.'

'But——'

'She has also been ill—you must see that,' Polly added.

Through all this Serena had sat motionless, speechless, but undeterred, the man still turned to speak to her again.

He must have changed his mind, though. Before Polly could say, 'Go away' again, and she had intended to, quite forcibly, he went.

'Eclair or macaroon, Serena?' Polly asked as uneventfully as she could.

There was no answer, and Polly saw that Serena still sat pinched and withdrawn, almost as though she was not there at all. Oh, heavens, Polly thought, how can I get her home, and if I do what can I say to him?—to Thorn?

But perhaps Serena would recover by then. It was an hour's drive to the Lime Tree turn-off, and the girl couldn't sit frozen all that time.

But Serena did. They travelled back without a word, travelled very slowly, Polly ekeing out the journey as long as she could in the hope that Serena would snap out of whatever she was in.

But Serena arrived at the house behind the stand of peppercorns in the same dazed state as she had shown in the coffee shop, and Polly knew that her only chance now was to get her to her bedroom and lay her down, perhaps administer a mild sedative. She only prayed that Thorn Clemance would not come on the scene.

At first she believed she was going to be lucky. She got the girl to her room without meeting anyone, put her on the bed, gave her a safe medication, and drew up a rug.

'Try to rest, Serena,' she whispered, and went out and shut the door.

But when she returned to her car it was to find that Thorn Clemance had left his lab, and that he was busily bundling up her bags and clothes to take to her room.

'I can do that,' Polly said a little too hurriedly, and he gave her a quizzical look.

'Something you don't want me to see? Some risqué dress, perhaps?'

'Don't be ridiculous!' she snapped.

'I quite like risqué dresses . . . on the right person. For all your young naïve look, Polly Kendall, I rather think you could wear a risqué dress.' He shot her that long green glance again.

'Let me have them.' Unceremoniously Polly grabbed the clothes from him and started down the passage. Surely, discouraged like that, the man would not follow her.

But Thorn did follow. He came with a second armful he had taken up . . . but he only came as far as Serena's door. Then something must have occurred to him.

'Mrs Ramsay said Serena's been asleep all morning,' he said. 'Then it's high time she stirred.' He put the clothes down on a small dropside table.

'Leave her alone!' In spite of herself, Polly's voice was sharp, even shrill. She knew as soon as she had called out that her injunction would have the opposite effect.

'What is this?' He did not ask it of Polly, he seemed to ask it of the closed door, a door he had crossed to and now opened.

He went inside.

Miserably Polly followed him and stood beside him as he sat on the bed beside the awake but unawake Serena.

'Come out of it, Serena,' he said. 'Come back to us! You've slept far too long.' To Polly he snapped: 'Don't just stand there doing nothing, get Mrs Ramsay to make some coffee—hot, sweet, strong.'

'It would be wrong,' answered Polly unhappily. 'I've already given her a sedative.'

'You *what*?'

'A sedative. Only a mild one.'

'But why?' he demanded.

'She had a—condition.'

'Just now?'

'No.'

'Then when?'

'Some time before.'

'How long before?' he persisted.

Polly muttered: 'Over an hour.'

'But an hour ago you were in Sydney, weren't you?'

'Yes.'

'Then don't tell me that——'

'Yes, I am telling you that. I took her with me. But I think' . . . Polly said in relief, looking down on the girl . . . 'she's coming round again.'

Serena was. The cloud in her violet eyes was clearing. She was losing her frozen look.

'Hullo, Thorn,' she smiled quite normally. 'Hullo, Polly. I just felt like a sleep.'

'Yes, and sleep some more, pet,' said Thorn. 'Look, I'll draw the blind, and we'll shut the door.' He was doing it as he spoke.

But the moment the door was shut behind them, he turned furiously on Polly. Before she realised it she—and he—were in her room, and the door there was being firmly closed.

His big hands were taking her upper arms and they were not gentle. He even went to shake her before he realised what he was doing and stopped.

'Now tell me,' he ordered angrily, 'tell me everything. I'm listening, Miss Kendall. Begin.'

CHAPTER THREE

POLLY made a movement to extricate herself, and to her surprise Thorn Clemance let her go. He even stepped back a pace from her and folded his arms. But his eyes were those narrowed green slits again as they watched her.

'I took your—I took Serena with me,' Polly began.

'Against my emphatic orders?'

'Yes. I'm sorry.'

'You're sorry!' he exclaimed.

'Very sorry. You see, she——' But Polly stopped herself. It really was her own fault, she reasoned; she should not have listened to Serena, she should have brought her back however hard the girl had begged. But she had not brought her, so why blame Serena now, and why try to defend herself? Anyway, this angry man would never listen.

'I failed to carry out your directions,' she told him. 'I ignored your orders. I'm responsible for Serena's condition. Now perhaps you'll change your mind about me.'

'Change my mind?'

'Let me go. I'm not suitable for this job—you must see that.'

'I told you before that it was Serena you had to suit, not me. Evidently you are suiting her.' His voice was dry.

'But you have the final authority.'

'Oh, yes' ... with a cool acceptance that maddened Polly ... 'I have that. And I say you will remain.'

'But if I don't wish to remain?'

'You still will, I think. Where else could you go?'

'There are other situations,' she pointed out reasonably.

'Not so many. There's a recession just now. Anyway, among those few offering there would be fewer still including accommodation, and I believe' ... his eyes dropping significantly to the garments he had put on her bed ... 'you've burned your bridges behind you as regards a roof over your head, you've given up your flat.'

... You jolly well know I have, Polly fumed to herself, this is what this interview is all about, the fact that I didn't comply with your order when I allowed your wife to go to Sydney with me. But she said nothing, only waited.

'Also,' she heard him saying in an almost indifferent voice, 'I don't think you've read your contract fully.'

'Contract?' she queried.

'When you took this job. Oh, yes, you signed an agreement. In future before you write your name, read the small print.'

Polly, who could not remember signing anything, did not answer. I could have done it, she thought, I was in a state of mind when I could have done anything.

'Was there small print?' she asked him.

'Very much so.'

'Referring to my——'

'Referring to your conditions of employment,' he

nodded. 'I'm sorry, but you're more or less tied to me for some time.'

'Tied?' she echoed.

'That's what I said.' He put on a sympathetic face. But at once the mock sympathy was brushed off. 'What happened?' he demanded.

'Happened?' she queried.

'For you to return a girl in that condition.' He jerked his head in the direction of Serena's room.

'Everything was going well,' Polly said. 'Serena was like an excited child.'

'She always is.'

'She helped me with my clothes, behaved so perfectly it seemed mean not to reward her, so——'

'So?'

'We went to a coffee shop. I thought there was no harm in that.'

'And someone recognised her, and came across.' Thorn beat her to it.

'Yes. He called her Renie. As soon as he said it, I noticed a change in her.'

'What sort of change?'

'She seemed—frozen.'

'Like she is now?'

'Yes.'

'So you brought her home?'

'After I told him—the person—to leave.'

'Did you do that?' He was looking at her enigmatically.

'Of course.'

He looked at her again, a long look now, then he spoke again, and his voice was much milder.

.'What was he like, this fellow?'

'Slick, flashy. I've never cared for the type.'

'So you sent him off and brought her home.' Thorn Clemance mulled that over, then he actually grinned. '*Not* such bad marks for you after all, Polly, taking into consideration it was not your fault that Serena was there in the first place.'

'What?'

'Oh, yes, I guessed that all along. Serena, I would say, concealed herself in your car, then popped up when it was too late to return her.'

Polly looked at him in indignation. 'You knew that all along, yet you put me through this examination?'

He shrugged. 'It keeps you on your toes, makes you less complacent.'

'I'm far from complacent! Also I consider that if you can cross-examine me like that, then I'm at least entitled to a few answers from you.' Before he could refuse or exclaim, Polly demanded: 'Why are you protecting Serena like this? Why are you making a prisoner of her? Why are you so restrictive, prohibitive, denying, subjugating?'

'Phew!' He pretended to wipe his brow at her words. Then he answered meaningly: 'I have to, seeing you're incapable.'

'I don't want to be capable, if it means being like that.'

'Being like me, you mean.'

'Yes. Concern is one thing, but captivity is another. She might as well be in a gaol!'

'Keep going,' he invited coolly.

'You're going about things the wrong way. I know it's none of my business——'

'It isn't,' he agreed.

'But you can't stifle her like this. You can't put her
in a drawer and turn the key. Do you know what she
said to me? "Thorn never stops watching me ...
guarding me ..." She even said : "He dusts me." Look,
she's an adult woman. She can't live like that.'

'Yet she's going to,' he broke in calmly, 'for some
time yet.'

'Some time yet——?'

'And *you* are going to help me. Well' ... a shrug
... 'so much for that. *Not* such bad marks for you
after all. You handled that flash, slick fellow like an
expert. Perhaps you'll do even better in your next
test.'

'*W-what?*'

'I'm going on a mountain safari,' he explained, 'and
I'm taking you and Serena with me. There's a certain
root specimen that I need for my next experiment,
and rather than leave you and Serena here, I propose
to take you along. It will only be a matter of three
days.'

'You don't trust leaving Serena with me?'

'I think,' he altered, 'Serena will benefit from a
change.'

Polly wasn't so sure. A safari seemed to her something that would *not* appeal to Serena. Surrounded
here at Lime Tree by nature at its most lush, Serena
very noticeably took small interest. No, Serena was
essentially a people person, not a nature-lover, and
Polly half smiled to herself.

Thorn saw the smile, but did not comment on it.

'We shall be away two nights,' he said, 'camping,
of course.'

Polly began to feel even less sure of Serena; she

simply could not see that hothouse flower curled up in a sleeping bag.

'Serena——' she began uncertainly.

'Will be bored to tears, I know that. But she would be bored here too. So at least she'll have a different background.'

'Yes.' But Polly still said it uncertainly.

'Anyway, I've decided on it.'—(And what you say is done.)—'I'll rely on you to see she brings the right clothes. You understand what I mean?'

'I do, but does Serena possess them?'

'Lend her some of yours as she loaned you hers. I see' . . . looking down . . . 'you have same flannelette offerings here.' He took out a pair of winter pyjamas and dangled them.

Embarrassed, Polly said hurriedly: 'Yes, I'll see to that.'

'And see to yourself at the same time. I know the kind of things that Serena has been pressing on you.' He moved further along the bed and this time hauled out and held up a pale pink concoction that had been peeping from underneath Polly's pillow. 'Don't let it go to your head.' His voice was dry.

'Really, Mr—I mean Thorn——'

He smiled crookedly at her correction, then mouthed a cool: 'Sorry if I've embarrassed you.'—But he was not sorry, Polly knew.

'Neck to toe for the bush,' he advised, 'and not too much. After all, we're only going for two nights.'

'Yes, Thorn,' Polly said tightly.

'We'll leave in the morning. Serena should be completely recovered by then. Mrs Ramsay will pack our provisions, I'll see to the tents and sleeping bags. You will see to the————'

'Neck to toes,' Polly came in before he could.

He gave another of his crooked grins and left the room.

Serena, out of her sleep, out of whatever trauma she had suffered as a result of her city encounter, was not, as Polly had anticipated, at all enthusiastic about the safari idea.

'I don't think I'll like camping.'

'It's lovely, Serena,' Polly enthused. 'A big moon, silver stars, the rustle of leaves.'

'Beetles, mosquitoes, queer shapes in the shadows of the trees.'

'But all good fun from the warmth of your sleeping bag. About sleeping, Serena, you can't take any of your pretty things, it's to be strictly neck to toe, and ... wait for it ... flannelette.'

'What? Oh, no, Polly!'

'Sorry, Serena, that's Thorn's orders for the bush.'

'I don't want to go to the bush. Besides, I've nothing like that. Like neck to toe and flannelette.'

'But I have. And seeing I accepted a loan from you, you're to accept a loan from me.'

'Flannelette! Probably pink!'

'Very pink,' Polly smiled. 'But look at it this way, at least the safari will be a diversion.'

'I'd sooner stop home and read a magazine,' said Serena sulkily.

'It's for two nights only, and anyway, Mr Clemance has spoken.'

'Yes,' said Serena unenthusiastically. She added: 'With luck it will rain and Thorn will have to put us in a hotel.'

'He's taking the tabletop with a roll-on waterproof roof,' Polly told her.

Serena grimaced.

The next morning Polly took Serena's three bags and her own overnight grip to the tabletop to be packed along with the tents, sleeping equipment, camp oven and tinned provisions.

Thorn Clemance raised his brows over the number of bags, but did not say anything except a grudging: 'So long as the contents are as ordered.'

'They are,' said Polly confidently, for she had stood beside Serena as the girl had packed.

They were soon on the Great Western Road, this time taking the steep rises of the upper Blue Mountains. It had rained during the night and a sweet, wet, herby smell rose from the valleys each side of them. Woodsmoke wreathed from the cottages dotting the hills and gullies and making misty patterns in the faintly blue air.

Somewhere after Blackheath Thorn turned into a deep valley. They went for several miles through a long channel of trees, and then he took a rough, narrow earth track.

Serena, sitting in the middle of the front seat because she disliked the wind, looked less enthusiastic than ever until she glimpsed a tent in the middle of the clearing at the end of the track.

'Someone else,' she said happily at the exact same time as Thorn said unhappily: 'Damn!'

But whoever the tent belonged to made no appearance . . . then.

Because there was nowhere else to go, and since the clearing was sufficiently ample for a dozen campers,

Thorn reluctantly drew up the tabletop. He fixed the beds, stacked the provisions, strung up, on Serena's request, a hammock between two handy gums, then wasted no time in descending to the bottom of the valley to search for his specimens.

Polly, torn between doing likewise, for she longed to scramble down and explore for herself, or looking after her charge, sighed and found a camp stool and sat beside the girl now swaying to and fro. If Serena followed her normal procedure she would soon slip off to sleep, Polly hoped, and at least she could take a quick look around.

But it was Polly who slept.

It must have been the change of air or the dancing pattern of the leaves that mesmerised her, for all at once everything was weaving, and after that she drifted off.

She awoke with a start, and saw that she must have slept for some time, for there were long shadows on the ground that had not been there before.

The birds sang differently, too, a more muted end-of-the day song, and among the deeper stands of the gums purple shades were already blotting out the blue-green of the thick foliage.

Polly got up ... then saw that the hammock was empty and that Serena had gone.

She would probably be in her tent deciding which of Polly's night offerings was less pink and less neck to toe, Polly smiled. She crossed to the sleeping accommodation that Thorn had fixed.

'Serena !' she called.

There was no reply.

After going into all the tents to make quite sure,

Polly came out baffled. She felt certain Serena would not go exploring, she was not fond of the bush, had said so on numerous occasions, so *where*?

Everything in the camp seemed the same as before, nothing altered, nothing taken. Unless—unless Serena, suddenly rebellious, just as she had been when she had hidden herself in Polly's car, had grabbed her handbag and set off to Blackheath. Shops fascinated Serena. Passing people did. Here there were neither. Even the other camper was nowhere in sight. Yes, Serena could have done that, she could have taken the opportunity of Polly's sleep to tackle the rough road to town. The village was some miles away, but Serena would never consider that. She simply would feel an impulse, then act on it, even though the end of day was setting in, night coming fast.

Polly stood undecided for a few minutes, and even as she gnawed at her lip in anxiety the last shred of the sun went over the horizon.

She could not alert Thorn, she did not even know which way he had gone, she only knew he had descended the valley.

But . . . and Polly hurried to where she had last seen him leaving the clearing . . . she could try a cooee. For Serena, for Thorn, it did not matter.

'Cooee, cooee!' she shouted at the top of her voice. 'Cooee!'

She was rewarded at once, but not by Thorn Clemance. Serena appeared at the flap of the one-man tent that both Serena and Thorn had spoken of . . . in different words . . . only some time before.

Behind her stood a man.

'What are you calling out for, Polly?' Serena asked.

'Thorn will only come when he's ready—he always does. Polly, this is Rod Enderley. When you stayed asleep like you did, I had to find someone to talk to. And it was Rod.' Serena turned to the man and smiled.

'How are you, Polly?' The man behind Serena stepped forward to acknowledge Polly. 'I'm indeed Rod Enderley, and I was as glad to talk to Serena as she insists she was glad to talk to me. I'm afraid I'm not quite the same as that fellow who only wanted to talk to the trees.'

'Did he really?' asked Serena with interest.

'Well, so went the song.'

They both laughed.

But Polly did not laugh. She could hear steps climbing up from the valley, and she knew it would be Thorn. Well, this man, anyway, this Rod Enderley, was not flashy and slick, and Serena was certainly not frozen, either, but positively glowing.

But would it make any difference? Polly felt that any male would not win Thorn Clemance's approval or friendship. For a husband who lived a bachelor life ... or tried to appear to? ... he had a very positive streak.

The steps were coming closer.

As Thorn Clemance reached the top, Polly turned from Serena and Rod and silently waited, unconscious that her hands were clenched. Behind her Serena and Rod waited, too.

But as soon as Thorn was in sight, Serena greeted him.

'Thorn darling,' she called, 'look what I found in the other tent. His name is Rod Enderley, and he's a doctor. He took time off from mumps and tonsils and came to talk to trees instead. Or that's what he said. Only, the same as with me, he's finding it boring, so we've both been talking to each other.'

For a few moments Thorn did not respond, though that could have been to catch his breath, it had been a steep ascent and he was laden with specimens.

Then he put the spoil down and said quite pleasantly: 'How do you do, Rod.' Another pause, then, still pleasantly ... too pleasantly? ... 'And all this occurred, I suppose, while our Miss Kendall either wandered off or slept.'

'Slept,' said Polly as pleasantly back to him.

He accepted that, he did not even flash her that narrowed green look of his, tighten his long mouth, but Polly knew it was not to stop at that.

She watched him showing the doctor his specimens, explaining their ultimate purpose, she watched Rod Enderley, medically alerted, evincing deep interest, Serena coming in whenever she could think of something to say.

She turned, and went across to their own camp. Bad marks again, she accepted, beginning the evening meal, the pumping of the lamps. She could only hope that the close proximity of the two camps would prevent Thorn from putting on a reckoning with her, something like he had staged last night. She felt she could not take that again, not in public.

She was spared. When Thorn eventually crossed, Serena and Rod Enderley came with him, and the young doctor carried an armful of his own provisions.

'We're dining foursome,' Thorn announced, and he lit the fire.

There were no recriminations, just pleasant chat-

ter. At least, Polly had to admit, Thorn Clemance
had been considerate to her in that.

It even appeared she was to escape altogether, for
later, after the doctor had pleaded weariness and returned to his own tent, Thorn still did not pursue
the matter.

Polly got Serena to bed ... Serena to her surprise
not grumbling any longer about flannelette; perhaps
it was the diversion of Doctor Enderley ... and was
about to unzip her own sleeping bag and creep in
when Thorn said quietly from the other side of the
fire: 'A word with you, please.'

Polly sighed, then pulled the utilitarian gown she
wore tighter around her, and joined him in the
shadows where he now awaited.

'*One* word?' she queried boldly—but still shiver-
ing a little in spite of her daring.

'There could be many—you damn well know that.
But this will do for now.'

'Yes?'

'Your Doctor Enderley——'

'Not mine,' she contradicted.

'Well, certainly not Serena's,' he said grimly.
'Enderley is the new medico at the newly opened
surgery at Apple Tree. He dropped it in conversation
tonight.'

'Should that mean anything to me?'

'Apple Tree is the nearest village to Lime Tree. I
believe I mentioned this before.'

'So?'

'So all this has to stop at once. See to it, please.'

'See to what?' she asked.

'It. Her and him.'

'Serena and——'

'Yes. Nip anything in the bud.'

'You mean stop it before it flowers?' Polly interrupted, momentarly forgetting that nothing could flower, not when Serena and this angry man beside her were husband and wife.

'Just do as I say,' he directed.

'But I don't understand you. Surely that should be your job.'

'Not when I'm telling you.'

'I think you really mean that what you say is done.' Polly went to step back to the camp, but her movement was not completed. All at once, she could not have said how, for she had not seen him step forward, he had hold of her.

'Very smart, aren't you?' he said a little thickly. 'You think you have all the answers, don't you? But' ... without warning ... 'have you an answer to this?'

Before she had a chance to draw away, his mouth came down on hers. It was completely unexpected, and as equally unplanned by him, she sensed, in spite of the fact that only he had instigated it. It was simply something that had happened between them, and the shock, to Polly, was not the actuality of it so much as her reaction, her trembling, her emotion. Most of all her response. For she was *not* pulling away, instead, instinctively, she was pressing forward, almost as though it was what she needed, must have. But she needed nothing, or if by some biological lore that she did not understand she *did*, then it must never be from him. Not only because she did not like him, but because she knew he was a married man. She hoped she was, and she tried to be, as modern as the next girl, but her childhood years, and her years with Uncle Ben, had emphasised one fact above all : the salient fact of marriage. Whatever kind of marriage these Clemances had, they still had it, and that, Polly knew intrinsically, was not, and never could be, for her. Pulling away, she braced herself, then put both her hands against his chest and pushed.

Thorn released her at once. He released her so abruptly that for several moments she swayed. He made no effort to steady her.

'Go back to your virginal sleeping bag, little one,' he almost yawned.

'And you, Mr Clemance?'

'I'll go to mine, too. Where else?'

'Well, I should have thought that you——'

'Yes?'

'It doesn't matter.' Not wanting to be questioned, Polly hurried across to her bed. After she had got into the bag and zipped it up she heard him doing the rounds of the encampment, seeing to lights, fires. Then she heard him, too, zipping his bag. Through it all Serena slept.

Polly did not know what time she awakened, what awakened her. She only knew that at some period she drowsily opened her eyes, and the next moment, shocked from sleep, she was out of the bag and on her feet.

The camp was ablaze.

Only a corner of Thorn's carefully arranged site was so far affected. Polly assured herself of this in a second urgent glance. But the involved part was the danger part, the isolated section where Thorn had cautiously placed their cooking equipment: the portable stove, the heater, the burner—the liquid fuel. He had positioned them scrupulously, but little good it had done him. The area now was alight, and in the centre of it, evidently struck dumb in terror, moved a silent Serena.

Polly could not believe it. Serena always slept: she had slept like a child earlier tonight in her padded bag. Polly had heard her deep breathing, and envied her. She herself had been restless for hours after she had returned from her interlude with Thorn. But now their sleeper was awake, desperately awake as she fluttered as a firefly would have fluttered between the fast encompassing flares.

Polly stepped closer, and it did not help her when she saw that the utilitarian, fireproof pyjamas she had watched Serena pack were not on the girl any more and that instead she wore a flimsy, ignitable gown.

What had happened? How had the fire begun? Why was Serena out of her sleeping bag and why was she dressed like that?

But there was no time for wonder now. Polly did the only thing she could think of: she screamed. She put everything into that scream, she made it as long and as loud as she could. She was still shouting out as she dragged their demijohn of water across and threw it over the blaze.

The screams had immediate response. Two responses. One from Thorn, who was out of his bag and on his feet in seconds. One from the doctor who was close behind him.

The grass around the camp was now ablaze. A piece of bark had entrapped a floating ember and was be-

ginning to light a tree. Because the tree was a euca-
lypt, the oil in the leaves hurried the ignition into an
exploding flame.

But this was noticed only by Polly; the men's attention was on Serena, Serena still moving like a firefly
in the red glow.

In one spontaneous movement they both stepped
towards her, but it was the doctor's arms that caught
her first, and Rod Enderley's hands that subdued the
flames that had started to lick at her nightdress.

He beat at the ignited material with his bare fists,
then he rolled Serena to the ground, rolling himself
with her, and after that he began rotating her back-
wards and forwards, upwards and downwards, forc-
ing out the heat. In minutes it was all over, and only
a thick pall remained.

Now Thorn came in. He said gruffly: 'I'll take
over.'

'No, I will.' Rod Enderley spoke with a quiet de-
termination. 'I know what to look for. After all, I
am a doctor.'

. . . But I'm Serena's husband. Surely Thorn would
answer that, anticipated Polly, extinguishing the
small flare in the tree. But Thorn didn't. Instead he
stood silent, and then, with a visual effort, he stepped
back. Rod Enderley began a careful examination of
Serena. He finished at last by cupping her hand in his
as he checked her pulse.

'Only shock,' he said cheerfully at length, 'and that
quite slight. Not even a burn or char. It's a miracle
in that flimsy gear that she didn't go up in a burst.'

'Yes,' said Thorn grimly, and he gave Polly a quick
look.

Polly moved away. She wondered again how the fire had begun and how Serena had come to be in the middle of it. Then she saw a billycan filled with water on the charred ground, and guessed that Serena had intended to surprise them with early morning tea. Poor child, her plans had gone astray.

But how did she come to be dressed as she was? Polly herself had supervised Serena's packing very assiduously, she had been afraid not to, she had even checked on the despised pink offering that Serena had worn earlier tonight but now was not wearing. Then, in spite of the serious situation, Polly began to smile. No doubt the minx had hidden her pretty things *inside* the sensible things, and when the idea of early tea had occurred had quickly changed.—Almost changed her life for death as well, Polly thought, sobered again.

Instinctively she took the billycan over to the small kerosene stove they had brought and finished what Serena had disastrously begun. When she had brewed the tea, she put a steaming mug in everyone's hands.

Serena and Rod said a grateful thanks, but Thorn did not speak.

They drank in silence for a while, then Polly noticed that the bush was fast becoming less dark.

'What time is it?' she asked.

Neither of the men had a watch handy, but both had an answer.

'Fairly near sun-up by that first buttering,' indicated Doctor Enderley of a faint primrose glow.

'It will be dawn in ten minutes,' Thorn judged.

'I knew morning would not be long,' Serena said unhappily, 'and that's why I thought I'd make tea for everyone, but instead I made——'

'You made a mess,' said Thorn.

'But everything's all right now,' Rod Enderley said comfortingly to Serena. He put an arm gently around her waist.

Polly saw Thorn watching him, and she was not surprised at his quick: 'It is, but it might not have been. Several years ago lives were lost in just such a fire as this, thousands of acres of superb forest were devastated, villages, houses, bridges scorched beyond repair. Fires in these heights leap from mountain top to mountain top in minutes. They run up trees. A bush can be lit up six miles in advance, it can——'

'I think,' broke in the doctor sharply, his glance on the shaken Serena, 'we'd better get this little lady to bed for the morning.' There was a challenge in his voice and in the look he gave Thorn.

At once Thorn accepted the challenge. 'Impossible,' he said, 'we're moving out.'

'Moving out?'

'We're going home.' Thorn paused, then added: 'Now.'

'But——'

'We're leaving immediately, Doctor Enderley. I consider it would be best.'

'And I consider it would be inadvisable.' Rod Enderley's voice was raised.

'Then I'll give her one hour while I finish my collecting. One hour, no more. Take Serena across to the sleeping quarters, Miss Kendall, and after you get her into her crib for a short break, start packing for our return.'

Polly said uncertainly, her sympathy with Serena

and the doctor: 'If you still felt like gathering more data again, Thorn, then I'm sure I——'

'That you can cope? No, thank you. You've coped enough already. Just do as I say. Get ready to go.' His voice was final.

As Polly obeyed his order, she saw Thorn turn to the doctor. 'I appreciate what you've done, and would do, but we'll be all right.' It was anything but a gracious gesture, but at least Rod had been thanked, not reprimanded in front of everyone as she had, she thought resentfully.

For all her resentment, though, Polly tucked Serena in, then began packing the things that had barely been unpacked. When she looked around she saw that Serena was quietly weeping.

'Don't fret, darling,' Polly coaxed.

'I can't help it, Polly, everything I do is wrong. I did want to surprise you all, prove to you that I'm not the helpless child you all think I am.'

'*I* don't think of you as a child, Serena. A child wouldn't have thought about a glamorous negligee. Why did you do it? And when?'

'I did it because I like things that are lovely, I've had enough of things that are not. As for when, I waited till you weren't looking.'

'Oh, Serena, Serena, what's Thorn going to do with you?' sighed Polly.

'What he's doing now, I expect. But he's told me it won't be for much longer.'

Packing cups and plates, Polly asked carefully: 'What won't be for much longer, Serena?'

There was no reply, and when Polly looked round Serena had characteristically drifted off.

Thorn had agreed to let Serena sleep for an hour, and he had already availed himself of his time allotment and gone down the valley.

With sudden daring, and feeling, anyway, that a doctor's supervision should be enough for the sleeping Serena, Polly decided to descend, too. After all, she had never really experienced these valleys, her stay in Sydney had been strictly Sydney, never its blue beckoning heights. Eagerly she started down.

It was glorious in the bush. Polly had not known that Australian woods were so beautiful. Tree ferns rose on every side, fallen trunks were covered with luminous mosses, and the ground gave up a sweet, aromatic tang.

Thorn had set out before her, and lingering as she did in the lovely surroundings, it was some time before Polly reached the valley bed, and the sight of Thorn on his knees and carefully coaxing out a root.

She came up to him silently, but just as she neared him she stepped on a stick, and its snap alerted him. He looked up immediately.

'What's wrong now?' he demanded.

'Nothing. No fire. No trauma. I simply came down.'

'Leaving those two up there together?' His voice was sharp.

'Well,' said Polly, disgusted, 'the doctor hasn't left yet, and neither has Serena.'

'I asked you *leaving those two up there together*?'

'Yes, Mr Clemance, if you must have it chapter and verse. Serena and Rod Enderley are up there together. Serena is asleep, Rod is tinkering with his car engine, but actually, I suppose, they're still there together. And why not, Mr Clemance? Oh, I know I'm supposed to watch Serena but never to question, still, why not? You can't——'

'I can't guard her?' Thorn angrily forestalled Polly. 'I can't tie her up? Restrict her? "Dust her", as you said? Well, I damn well am trying to, and I wasn't doing too badly until you came.'

'Meaning,' leapt Polly eagerly, 'that you *are* finding me unsatisfactory?'

'That would be the understatement of my life!'

'Meaning then that I can——'

'Go? Leave? Resign? Oh, dear me, no.' His thinned smile was insincere.

'But——' she began.

'The small print on a contract, remember? Binding, incidentally, for me as well.'

'Then I release you.'

'But I,' said Thorn, 'don't release you.'

He waited a moment, then he actually ... and ridiculously, Polly thought ... spread his big arms in a pax gesture. 'You stay on,' he told her magnanimously. 'But just as a matter of interest——'

'Yes?'

'Do you always cause trouble like this wherever you go?' he demanded.

'Trouble? I?'

'First it was sharks, then it was night hallucinations' ... Polly's cheeks flamed ... 'then it was that Sydney caper.'

'Now I suppose you're blaming me for Serena's near-disaster?'

He did not answer that, instead he continued: 'Next it was Enderley. You did hear me last night, I presume, when I told you where the doctor lived?'

'I couldn't help but hear you. Apple Tree.'

'Which is one village away from Lime Tree and a village too close. Good lord, you must have noticed, as I did, Serena's reaction to the fellow.'

'He seems a very nice fellow,' she commented reasonably.

'And only a kilometre or so away from Lime Tree. Did she realise that, do you think? *Did* Serena?'

Polly answered: 'I don't know. What if she did? You don't think she'd leave you for him, do you? You're not that unsure of her, are you?'

'The only thing I'm sure of in Serena is her own unsureness.'

'Then the way you're going on with her will scarcely cure that.'

'No? Then what will?'

'Your—well, your love for her, your fond affection.' A pause. 'Your husbandly trust.'

There was a sudden silence in the valley bed, a silence as unmistakable as that silence that comes before a storm. Then——

'My *what* trust?' Thorn Clemance fairly shouted; Polly felt sure it could be heard for miles.

He had risen from his haunches and now he towered above her. He took her arms in his and held them, and his clasp was steel.

'My what?' he shouted again.

'Your husbandly trust, I said.'

'But isn't that usually the prerogative of a husband?'

'Yes.'

'Well, why in hell should I be picked out?'

'You're Serena's husband.'

'Why should you think that? Have I ever said so? Did I introduce her to you as my wife? Did I sign you on as my wife's companion? Did I ever use the word wife?'

'No, but I naturally gathered ... I really mean I never thought of anything else ...' Polly blurted dazedly. She was remembering a dozen things at once. Like the same name, Clemance. Like the same background, Lime Tree. Like the jealous way a husband would guard his wife. Like——

They all added up to one thing: a man and a woman joined in marriage. At least she had thought so.

And yet, her thoughts ran on, there had been other things, too. The need for someone else ... for Polly ... there as well, almost as if it had been a conventional requirement.—'I myself don't live in except when Thorn especially requests it,' Mrs Ramsay had said. Later: 'Thorn's a stickler. Now Gil——'

Most of all, and to her dismay Polly felt her cheeks burning, was the evidence of those two rooms. Two rooms for one man and his wife.

Almost as if she had spoken her thoughts aloud, Thorn Clemance had moved to her and his first words continued from her thoughts.

'Look at me, Miss Kendall, *look at me*, tell me what you see.'

'I—I don't understand you.' Polly tried to retreat a step, but he advanced, and at once they stood barely an inch apart.

'I think you do understand, though. I think you see a man who is no half-measures man. I think you see a man who would not be put off with subtleties, evasions and half-truths from any woman he made his wife. I think you see a man who would demand an entirety, a fulfilment, a conclusion, a completion.' A pause. 'I think you see a man who would be demanding four, not eight walls.

'Now do you understand?'

He was half smiling, half taunting her, and Polly searched desperately but could find no answering words.

'Did I appear to you the kind who would put up with that sort of marriage?' he finished at last.

'No ... I mean ...'

'Then why did you think it?'

'What else could I think? You never told me. You never explained.'

'It shouldn't have been needed. Not needed, anyhow, by you.'

'Why me?'

'Because you're not a half-measures woman yourself. I was aware of that the first day I met you. I sensed the same in you as I knew already in myself. An entirety, a conclusion, a completion. I saw—this!'

Without warning, the same as last night, he wrapped his big arms around her, and the clasp was so tight she could not move.

'You are a very desirable woman,' he said, 'your man back in England must have been mad to let you go. From the first moment by the river I thought that, and from that first moment by the river I haven't been able to get you out of my mind. Now I'm finding I can't get you out of my senses. The scent of you, the warmth of you, the——'

He stopped talking, but his hands began moving, and as he followed the swell of her breasts through her jacket with his exploring fingers she felt her heart thudding, and she knew he must be feeling her heart beat as well.

She knew that his breath was quickening and his muscles firming, just as she knew that her own body was moving instinctively towards his.

When his lips closed down on hers, her own clung back. He held the kiss a long moment, then he stopped and looked down at her and gave a small laugh.

That small laugh dispersed something. Without moving from him Polly felt something within her recoil.

It had been a laugh of triumph, she interpreted. It had to be. For all that Serena was not Thorn Clemance's wife, he still had Serena by him. What was his answer to that?

Now Polly felt a hate rising in her, hate for him for his using of her; hate for herself for her response. But most of all a hate for his practised mastery of the situation ... and mastery of Polly Kendall.

But curiously, for all her anger, Polly still stood as though magnetised as the man slowly and deliberately began running his sensual fingers through her hair, first at the temples, then at the nape of her neck. Her pulses moved with his as he traced the line of her slender backbone, as he explored the hollow of her throat, as his hands once more followed the swell of her breasts. Then she felt his hand at the neck of her shirt unbuttoning the shirt; then she felt the warmth of his fingers on her flesh.

'I haven't been able to get you out of my mind.' He started saying it all again but in an intimate whisper now. 'I haven't been able to get you out of my senses. So what follows, Polly Kendall? Can you tell me that?'

He waited for her answer, but Polly was beyond words now and could not speak.

'I think from the response I felt in you just then,' he went on as she still remained silent, 'that you, too, will be facing that question very soon.' He looked deeply down at her.

Polly avoided his green gaze, then she shook her head as though to clear it. This was too preposterous, she was thinking. Did this man, this Thorn Clemance, really think he could reserve one woman yet play along with another? He had told her Serena was not his wife, and she believed him, but he had still made no attempt to explain Serena. Did he imagine he could get away with that?

'Who is Serena?' she asked, trying to pull away from him, only to be enfolded again.

'The widow of a cousin, Rollo Clemance,' he said shortly, and though it answered her question it did not elucidate a thing. It did not explain why Serena was at Lime Tree, why she was so jealously guarded, so tenderly kept. Unless——

Unless this man, in spite of his arms now tight around her, wanted his dead cousin's wife—for himself.

Unless she, Polly, was just a diversion for him, a means of filling in time, an entertaining dalliance until he was ready for the real thing . . . the real woman.

There were men like that; Polly had met them before herself. Why should this Thorn Clemance be any different? Why should Thorn be interested in average Polly Kendall and not beautiful Serena Clemance unless his interest was only a passing thing, something to relieve the boredom of waiting? For whatever other uncertainty Polly had harboured, she had never had any uncertainty about Thorn Clemance's waiting. Definitely the man was waiting. For what? For whom?

In spite of her chaotic thoughts Polly still stood there waiting herself, waiting for him to go on.

'Why is she here?' she heard herself asking tensely when he did not elaborate on what he had said.

'Who?' he asked.

'Why is Serena at Lime Tree with you?'

'But I told you—she's widowed.'

'But *why*?'

'Why, Polly?'

'Why is she here?' she insisted.

'I have my reason.'

'Which you don't intend to tell me.'

'No,' he answered, 'not yet.'

There was silence for a while. Polly broke it.

'I see,' she said. 'Well, it doesn't matter, because I think I know. I believe it's to do with the way you guard her, keep every other male ... and Rod? ... away.' Her voice was a little shrill.

'You're very discerning.' The shrillness had evidently not reached him. All at once he let her go. He even seemed to have forgotten what had happened just now. His face was that smouldering face he always wore.

'That's why Enderley must be stopped at once,' he said. 'You do understand that, Polly?'

'Oh, I certainly understand it ... now.' Polly had taken the opportunity of his slackened arms to step right away from him. 'I also think, in my new understanding, that we'd better return at once.' Her voice was sharp.

He looked questioningly at her, in his self-absorbing thoughts patently not following her, but when he found nothing in her face to tell him what she was thinking, he hunched his shoulders and collected his stuff.

They did not speak on the way up; the steep climb, anyway, would have prevented that.

When they reached the top, Rod Enderley had his own gear packed and was ready to leave, too. Serena was up and looking as though nothing had happened to her.

'Can I travel down with Rod?' she asked Thorn. 'There would be more space then for your specimens.'

'You're coming with us,' was all Thorn's reply.

'But, Thorn——'

'Just get in, Serena. Yes, in the middle again. You complained about the wind on the way up.'

'There's no wind today. I think you're very mean, Thorn,' Serena pointed. 'I think you're making sure I don't get out.'

'Then think that.' He pushed her into the cabin, then nodded to Polly to sit beside her. He turned to Rod Enderley who was watching them. 'Goodbye,' he nodded curtly.

The doctor, patently taken aback by the cursory

treatment, began to say something that was not heard.

It was not heard because Thorn Clemance had already left the camp.

CHAPTER FOUR

THEY drove in silence until they had reached the village of Blackheath. Here Thorn drew up in front of the police station and announced that he was going in to report the fire.

'Was that necessary?' Polly questioned when he came back and they started off again. She asked it wonderingly, never obliquely, but he chose to take it as having some oblique inference.

'I prefer to do things the open way,' he said stiffly.

'Meaning?'

'You. You changed down there in the valley.'

. . . So he *had* noticed, Polly thought. Aloud she retorted: 'Are you always the same person yourself, Thorn? I would scarcely describe you as an open book.' She glanced meaningly at Serena, only to discover that the girl had drifted off once more. She slipped a cushion behind the deep gold head while she waited for Thorn's response, but when he spoke again it was not an answer.

'Serena has been under sedation for some time,' he said rather tersely of the sleeping girl.

'Then she *has* been ill?' Polly probed.

'No, not exactly. Look, let's drop it for a while.' His voice held a trace of weary appeal.

'Very well,' Polly conceded.

She sat silent as he began negotiating the sharp mountain bends. The scenery unrolling on each side of them was quite superb, but she scarcely saw it. Could this man be the same man who had pulled her so urgently to him only a short while ago? she wondered hollowly. He had first become this other man when she had questioned him about Serena, proving, she had thought then, thought again now, that she *was* only a diversion, a means of marking time until such time as a sleeping princess awoke.

That sounded fairytale, makebelieve, but there was no makebelieve in Polly's thoughts. She was convinced now that an awakening in Serena was what Thorn Clemance was waiting for. The girl was obviously ill at the moment, but when she was better Thorn Clemance wanted his cousin's widow for his own wife, and nothing, and no man, was going to stop him.

But meanwhile when the waiting grew tedious, he——

Polly's cheeks burned.

'I'm sorry about Serena's negligee instead of the neck to toe,' Polly offered some miles later.

Thorn shrugged. 'I knew it would be Serena's doing,' he said.

'Still I'm sorry. I should have re-checked.'

He merely gave another shrug, and the conversation lapsed.

As they ran over the foothills to the flats, Serena awoke.

'Is Rod in front or behind us?' she asked, at once dashing any hope that Thorn might have cherished of her already having forgotten the doctor.

Nonetheless Thorn asked falsely: 'Rod?'

'Rod Enderley. He camped near us. Is he?' Serena

peered behind them.

'He's well ahead,' Thorn lied.

'But I wanted to see him, to give him my address.'

'He has that.'

'You gave it to him, Thorn?'

'. . . Yes.'

'And did he give you his?'

'No. But you would know it already, of course?' Thorn asked slyly.

'No, I never thought to ask. Oh, why didn't you do it, Thorn?'

'Don't worry, Serena, he'll be enquiring.'

'You think so?' Serena's voice was eager.

'What do *you* think?' Thorn turned from the wheel and smiled winningly at her.

'I think he will,' Serena smiled back.

'Then don't worry, as I said. Don't worry, do you agree, Polly?' A quick, authoritative glance from the road.

'I won't worry,' Polly complied mechanically. She felt sure that the doctor would indeed enquire . . . *but that he would be politely but definitely put off*.

Serena accepted their assurances; she was very childlike in her belief in people, Polly thought. She felt she must know more about Serena, and about the husband who had died and of whom Serena never spoke. They would be difficult questions to ask, though, the girl seemed so delicately, even precariously, balanced. Perhaps Thorn . . . No, she had already tried, and been rebuffed.

They reached Lime Tree late in the morning, and at once Thorn Clemance began working on his specimens, but before that reminding Polly . . . when

Serena was not in earshot . . . of the nearness of Apple
Tree, of the close vigilance needed in the possibility
that Serena suddenly might take a liking to walking.

'She might even grow wings and fly there,' Polly
said coolly.

He gave her a remote look and simply answered:
'Watch her.'

Thorn need not have worried about either walking
or flying, for the Enderley contact, when it came,
was by telephone. And Serena was not there.

Polly, answering the ring, recognised the caller the
moment he asked: 'Serena?'

'No, it's Polly, Rod. It is Rod, isn't it?'

'Yes, Polly. I was wondering if I could speak to
Serena.'

'She's not around just now.' Polly was glad that
that was the truth, glad she did not have to stand
judgement as to whether the man could speak to
Serena. She gnawed at her lip, though. Why had
Thorn Clemance put her in such an invidious position? Then what if the next time he telephoned Lime
Tree, Serena answered herself?

'Oh.' The disappointment in Rod Enderley's voice
was very apparent.

He paused a moment, then asked Polly:

'When?'

'When what, Rod?'

'When can I talk to her, Polly?'

'I'm sorry, Rod, but I don't know. I mean it's not for
me to say, is it? I really mean . . . well, Rod, Serena
is—Serena *Clemance*. You knew that, of course.' It
was a dishonest thing to do, an unkind thing, but it
had been done, if unintentionally, to her, and it could

be a way out now, Polly thought wretchedly.

But it was not a way out. Rod Enderley said at once it his quiet voice: 'Oh, yes, I know she's *a* Clemance.'

'*A* Clemance?' picked up Polly.

'That's what I said.'

'. . . Serena told you.'

'She told me nothing, but a man . . . no, that should be *this* man . . . knew at once.'

'Knew what?' she asked.

'I knew at once that she was not Thorn Clemance's wife, Polly, if that's what you're babbling about.'

'Well, *I* didn't know,' said Polly, 'not until I was told.'

'Perhaps, but you weren't—hadn't——'

'Yes, Rod?'

'Fallen in love.'

Fallen in love. Polly thought that over a moment. Did Rod mean that love gave you an intuition you had not had before?

'Rod?' she heard herself asking again. 'Rod?'

'Yes, Polly, I said *fallen in love*.'

'In that short time!'

'It could have been shorter.'

'But Rod, you can't!' she protested.

'Why can't I? Look, Polly, tell me what goes on, what gives. What is Clemance trying to do? Stop something as natural as life itself? Because it won't work. I love the girl, already I love her. And I think in a very little while, if she doesn't love me already, then she will. Polly——' But the last word was to a dead line, for a shadow had come into the hall and Polly had put down the receiver in a hurry.

It was Thorn who had entered, and he stood at the

door with his big arms folded, his shadow long in front of him.

'That was an abrupt finish to a call,' he remarked.

'I didn't notice,' she shrugged.

'Of course you noticed, because you killed it. Who was it? But Enderley, of course.'

Polly did not reply, and he took the silence as agreement.

'Have there been previous calls?' he demanded next.

'None that I've answered,' Polly snapped.

'Then there've been none. I've had Ainsley monitoring the phone, so your answering today must have been a slip-up.'

Polly did not hear that last part, she was fuming at the fact that this man had instructed his secretary to spy on Serena, for spy, she thought, was the only word.

'You what?' she exclaimed aghast.

'I've had the phone checked by my secretary, so no calls have come through for Serena. That, of course, isn't to say she hasn't rung him.' A pause. 'Has she?'

'How should I know?'

'You should, because I employ you to know, pay you to know.'

'I can't be with her all the time, I can't——'

'You can't live her life,' he agreed. 'No, but you'd still know. Serena could never keep it to herself. Has he rung, suggested a meeting? Has she? A rendezvous could easily be arranged. You could drive her across to Apple Tree in your car, you could——'

'And reckon with you later?' broke in Polly.

He actually grinned at that, it was a brief smile but it was there.

'I see you have the right idea,' he approved.

'Of guarding Serena?'

'Of not wanting to face a reckoning with me.'

'No, thank you,' Polly said bitterly, 'I've had one already.'

'You have?' His brows rose steeply.

'Down in the valley.'

'You called that a reckoning?'

'It was my idea of one.'

'Then it was not mine,' he said in a low, furious voice, so angry that involuntarily Polly stepped back a pace.

Without another word he turned away from her.

A week went by, Thorn almost continuously in his laboratory, Serena going restlessly from one diversion to another, then suddenly . . . and Polly should have been alerted by the change . . . not needing a diversion any longer, just being a sweet amiable girl. But Polly, tired out by watching Serena, took the girl's welcome serenity as a sign that she had forgotten the mountain interlude, forgotten Rod Enderley, something, anyway, Serena could be expected to do, for she soon forgot everything. The peace was so welcome after Serena's recent restlessness that Polly embraced this acceptance with vast relief. She even decided to tell Thorn he could cancel his own watchfulness, cancel Ainsley's monitoring, when——

Mrs Ramsay had called out to a searching Polly that Mrs Clemance had left the house and gone down the garden.

'She's a changed person,' she beamed to Polly. 'Before she wouldn't settle for five minutes, but now, and I still can't believe it, she's got herself interested in flowers.'

'That's good. Growing or picking?'

'Neither. Wildflowers. Lime Tree has a lot of wildflowers. Not near the house, of course, but down towards the river.'

'That's fine then. The fresh air will do her good.'

Polly could not have said what urged her to go after Serena several days later when again the other girl was away, it was not the fact that Serena never returned with any flowers, she could have been studying them, not picking them, it was just a sudden feeling to follow her and see for herself.

Polly did see.

Rounding a corner of the bush beyond the last fence of the old home, she came upon Serena and Rod Enderley. They were some hundred yards ahead of her, and they were walking idly between the trees. Their arms were entwined.

At once Polly stepped back. She had no intention of joining them, in fact in her present confusion she had no real intention to do anything. Except, of course, report to Thorn. She would have to tell Thorn. It might have been Serena whom she had to suit, but it was Thorn who paid her. Thorn who told her what was expected of her. The guardianship of Serena was expected of her, so she must tell him at once.

Only she wouldn't: she knew that. Between the leaves of the shrub behind which she had hidden Polly could see Serena and Rod still walking together. Tears sprang to her eyes. She knew she could *not* tell.

Young lovers, she recognised, Serena and Rod were that.

Ironically it was that evening, Serena having gone early to bed, that Thorn spoke again of Rod Enderley.

'The incident seems to have passed over,' he said, well pleased.

'Incident?' asked Polly, pretending ignorance.

'The camping doctor and our difficult girl.'

'Oh—oh, yes.'

'You agree with me?'

'What's that? Oh, Serena and Rod? Of course. In fact I'd forgotten.' How easily a lie came when you felt deeply enough about it.

Thorn chuckled, obviously satisfied with himself.

'The whole bit will soon be over,' he said, making no sense to Polly, and he extended his big arms in a gesture of relief. 'I'm beginning to feel let off the leash at last. I'm even beginning to feel so confident that I'm considering allowing Serena out for a while. Why are you looking at me like that? It was you who wanted it.'

'Yes, but I never thought to hear such a thing from you.'

'Well, you're hearing it. Serena's Aunt Rebecca has been wanting her to stay with her for some time now, so to Aunt Rebecca's she'll go.' He added, with his usual quick decision: 'She'll leave tomorrow.'

'To where?'

'Brisbane. Aunt Becky lives there. She and her husband Claud are returning after a sojourn south, and want to take her with them. I've decided to change my mind regarding my first refusal and allow them to take Serena for a week or so.'

'Serena may not want to go.' Polly was thinking of two people walking arms entwined in the bush.

'But she's fond of Becky and Claud, and has complained many times of being bored here.'

'Not lately,' Polly said before she thought.

But Thorn was so confident he did not flash her his usual suspicious look.

'You can tell her,' he said, 'or shall I?'

'Am I to go, too?'

'No. I'd like you to, as an extra precaution, but it's a small car and there wouldn't be room. I thought I might send you up at the end, though, to fly back with her.'

'Then what do I do here?' asked Polly.

'How do you mean what do you do here?'

'I mean *here*. Whom do I look after?'

'You could try me,' he suggested.

'You would be the last person in the world who needed looking after!'

'You could be wrong, you know.'

A silence fell between them. Thorn broke it.

'I would sooner see you gone, and I admit it. You as well as Serena would be better away when Gil comes back.'

'Is he coming?' she asked.

'Yes.'

'But what difference can it make with me?'

'None at all—*I'll* see to that.' He looked at Polly levelly. 'I don't really know you, Polly, do I?'

'In what way?'

'In your way of dealing with——Gils.'

'Gils?' she queried.

'Men like my brother Gil.'

'Is Gil that different from you?'

'Yes, he is different.'

'You mean no entirety, fulfilment, conclusion, completion,' Polly said flippantly.

'You remember that?'

'. . . I hadn't forgotten.'

'Then don't forget this, either, when Gil comes.'

'Yes?'

'Gil is a woman's man.'

'Good for him!' Again Polly resorted to flippancy.

'But not good for you. For though Gil likes them all, he loves only one. Unfortunately he's not deeply aware of that yet. But it will come, have no two thoughts about that.' A pause. 'Now you can go and pack Serena's bag.'

Before Polly could answer him, he went out.

Polly was right, Serena was not enthusiastic over her break away.

'I don't want to go. Why do I have to? I don't think I will.'

'Thorn says your aunt and uncle are looking forward to it.'

'Then I'm not, and I know when I tell—when I——'

'Yes, Serena?'

'Nothing . . . nothing, Polly. I—I just don't want to go, that's all. Though——'

'*Yes*, Serena?' Polly asked once more, and a little suspiciously this time.

'Nothing, Polly. I told you—I'll go.' Serena gave an angelic smile.

The next day the car called, collected Serena and left. Polly waved the travellers off, then came back to the house. She wondered how she would occupy herself in the week or two that Serena would be away.—She wondered, apart from his practice, how Doctor Enderley would?

Had Serena told Rod? The way they had walked together that day Polly felt that Serena would not have left without doing so. Yet there had been so little time, and, as far as she knew, no opportunity.

That afternoon Polly chose the hour she had seen the couple in the bush and took the river track herself. Serena might not have got a message through and Rod might be there.

She walked quietly down the path, enjoying the late spring sun on her back. The woods, now emerged from the dun of winter, were trying out their pale green attire.

She came to the spot where she had seen Rod and Serena that day. The bush lay still and empty around her. She walked a little further, but still there was emptiness, no one to see. She found a rock and sat down.

It was pleasantly warm in the little thicket; scraps of blue sky came filtering through the trees in checkered patterns. Everything was still and a little drowsy. Even the birds were silenced, and any cricket song came only intermittently and delicately blurred.

Polly must have closed her eyes. She could not remember doing so, but she still must have, for all at once there was not just sleeping bush in front of her, there was somebody . . . a man.

She rose, greeting: 'Rod!' Then she saw it was not Rod Enderley, not anyone she knew. She tried to apologise, but before she could do so, the man came nearer and spoke.

He said: 'You're Cousin Serena—you have to be. I've been told about Serena's beauty, and by George, it's right!'

By this time he had stepped forward and taken both of Polly's hands in his. He said warmly: 'Serena, I'm Gil.'

Polly stood with her hands still in Gil Clemance's hands. She had not thought much about the younger Clemance, there had been no reason to think, but whenever he had come into the conversation, and she had formed a mental picture of him, it had been coloured by what Mrs Ramsay had said of him, what his brother Thorn had . . . Ainsley.

Mrs Ramsay had spoken tolerantly and affectionately, Thorn without tolerance and apparently no over-abundance of affection, but Ainsley had unmistakably adored him. Ainsley had even said: 'It was like that from the first time I came here.' Later she had added: 'You'll understand when you see Gil.'

Now Polly *was* seeing him, yet not quite knowing her own reaction, only being aware of laughing eyes, a full mobile mouth, most of all of a charm so immense it wasn't fair that it was encased in one man. He was like, yet unlike, Thorn Clemance. If you looked long enough and close enough you could tell they were brothers, but Gil was slimmer, much more boyish, more sparkling. His smile, and he was smiling now, reached out and captured you. It was infectious, that bright, bright smile of Gil's. Yes, Ainsley had been right. Seeing Gil, and at once being vividly aware of him, was inevitable. Inevitable, Polly recalled, had been Ainsley's own word.

Still holding her hands, Gil was carrying on with his Serena theme.

'Everyone told me Cousin Rollo had married a goddess, done the Clemances proud, but I only laughed, not believing a goddess would marry Rollo, yet now my laughter is over. Why did you, you glorious girl?'

'Why did I what?'

'Marry Rollo Clemance.'

'I didn't. Also, I'm not glorious. Finally,' Polly added, 'I'm also not Serena.'

'Not Serena?' he exclaimed unbelievingly.

'No. Name of Polly—Polly Kendall. Paid companion to Mrs Serena Clemance on Mr Thorn Clemance's orders, therefore on Mr Thorn Clemance's payroll. But just now not doing any work to earn my keep, because Mrs Clemance is not at home. She left this morning for Brisbane with an aunt and uncle.'

'They've taken her with them?'

'Yes, for a short break. I'm sorry.'

'Sorry?' he queried.

'Sorry you're disappointed.'

'Who said I was disappointed? Who could be disappointed with you left in her place?'

'You're very kind, but very wrong,' Polly smiled. 'I could never take Serena's place. Serena's a beauty.'

'I just called you one,' Gil pointed out.

'I had no competition,' she shrugged.

'Nor needed any. You're a very lovely girl, and good luck to Serena, may she stay away as long as she likes so long as you stay here.' The clasp of his hands tightened, and Polly, though intending to, did not pull away.

'So now,' Gil went on, 'as well as saying that Cousin Rollo did the Clemances proud, I'm saying that big brother Thorn has done Lime Tree proud.'

'In what way, Mr Clemance?'

'Employing you—and *Gil*, please, Polly. See, I'm already calling you that, darling,' he laughed.

'Really, Gil——' Polly tried to object.

'Yes, really. I've only met you a minute or so, but already I know.'

'Know what?'

He took his hands away from her hands to circle her with his arms instead.

'That's for you to find out,' he challenged.

'You're being absurd,' endeavoured Polly weakly. 'Besides, I've heard all about you.'

'That doesn't sound good,' he admitted. 'I can see I may have to work hard on you. I'll like that.'

'As you like gathering girls as well as specimens wherever you go?' Polly heard herself teasing quite fondly already. She tried to take a pull on herself. She shouldn't speak like that to the man now tightening his arm around her as they instinctively set out together through the woods ... another thing she should not permit. She tried halfheartedly to discourage him, discourage herself, but she had only gone a few steps when she realised she was incapable of reacting otherwise. Gil was simply, basically, unarguably that kind of charming, irresistible male. What had Thorn said? 'Gil is a woman's man.'

Yes, Gil was.

He was pretending now to ponder over her words

of gathering girls as well as specimens.

'Perhaps I have done that,' he frowned, 'but never any more. Not now.' He touched her cheek lightly. 'But who told you, Polly?' He pretended this time to think hard, and at last proclaimed triumphantly: 'Ramsay! She regularly despairs of me.'

'Yet loves you.'

'Of course. Everyone does.' An impudent grin.

'Your brother as well?'

'Old Thorn,' he shrugged.

'Not so old.'

'Not,' agreed Gil unkindly, 'that you'd notice. Tell me' ... stopping, and stopping Polly with him ... 'what do you make of Thorn?'

'Does anyone ever make anything of him? He seems to be completely self-sufficient.'

'Not like his brother, is that it? Well, I don't mind admitting I'm not. I need much more than I can provide for myself. But this isn't answering me. What do you make of Thorn?'

'Self-sufficient, as I said. Very thorough. A—a full measure man.' Polly had not meant to say that, it slipped through itself.

'A full measure man.' Gil thought that over a moment. 'Yes, I think I know what you mean. No punches pulled, no holds barred. A course travelled right to its end.'

'Is that bad?'

'Not bad, but possibly boring. Now I'm not like that at all. I like lightness, fun. You're both of those, I think, so I like you.' He gave her a quick unexpected kiss. 'No, I love you,' he corrected. 'I love you already.' He was outrageous, he was impossible, but Polly had to laugh.

They walked, arms entwined a moment, then Gil asked: 'What other reports did you have of this black sheep?'

'Only Ainsley telling me about you, and you were not black in her report.'

'Ainsley.' He was silent a moment. When he spoke he said a second time: 'Ainsley.'

Polly glanced up quickly and saw that his face was serious for a change. At once, seeing her eyes on him, he laughed again.

It was easy talking to Gil. Polly was not conscious, as she was with Thorn, of wondering what she should say next, she just let the words come. That Gil felt the same with her was very obvious. He kept up an interesting, amusing, too often much too personal flow of conversation that left no room for pauses.

'You never stop,' Polly managed to insert during that walk in the bush.

'I'm stopping now,' he pointed out, and he did. And kissed her again.

For a moment she did try to resist. This, she tried to tell herself, was simply too much. But the smiling eyes above hers brazenly teased affection back from her, and she found she could not.

'I feel I've known you all my life,' she said, defeated.

'You have,' he answered her. 'I've been waiting for you from the day you were born.'

By the time they got back to the house they could have been the old friends that Polly felt they were ... they could have been more than that. Only twice did the enchantment falter. The first time was when Ainsley came to stand at her office door at the end of her working day, the other was when Thorn was present later in the house. Gil, though trying to hide it, was patently in awe of his brother, Polly judged. He might call him 'old Thorn' ... 'not bad but possibly boring' ... but he still held him in an unwilling but very real respect. An attitude, Polly noted in exasperation, that Thorn seemed to take as his holy right. She was glad when the uncomfortable evening ended, and the trio broke up. She shut her bedroom door, then went to the window and looked out ... looked for a long time. She began thinking about Gil.

She remembered last year, and how she had believed her life began and ended with Steven. Now she knew it had not, that Uncle Ben had been right after all. He had said she had been a singer looking for a song, he had told her to find someone else to love. Well, Uncle Ben, she smiled into the darkness, perhaps I have.

In the days that followed it became apparent, even to a newcomer like Polly, that the fact of Gil back at Lime Tree, but making no attempt to leave again, was beginning to infuriate Thorn.

Gil reported this to Polly on one of their many walks together, Thorn cloistered in his lab, Ainsley presumably with Thorn, for Polly never saw her.

'Big Brother is beginning to make pointed remarks regarding my overstaying myself.' Gil kicked at a stone on their path.

'Are you, Gil?'

'Well, I suppose so. It's my job to collect what he wants, then market his findings.'

'And you can't do that here.'

'I wish I could.' Gil gave her a long look. 'It's time,' he went on, 'that Thorn took me in with him, gave somebody else this roving assignment.'

'That from a rover!' she smiled.

'Oh, I've enjoyed it,' admitted Gil. 'But I'm ready to step up now. I believed old Thorn was ready to accept me, he gave that indication. But then this Serena syndrome began, and he obviously doesn't want me around.' A pause. 'What gives there, Polly?'

'Gives?' she queried.

'What's in Thorn's cunning mind? Why is he harbouring Serena? Do you reckon my big brother has his eyes on her for himself?'

'She's very beautiful,' Polly faltered.

'*You* are beautiful, so it must be something more than that. Money, perhaps? Rollo could have left his young widow well heeled, and brother Thorn would be conscious of that fact.'

'Thorn would have plenty of money already.'

'Every man wants more,' Gil said.

'Do you?' Polly tried to put a laugh in her voice. She did not care for the conversation.

'Only more of you, Polly,' Gil answered at once. 'But until that can happen——'

'Yes?'

'Let's enjoy ourselves.'

'Aren't we now?' she asked.

'Not so much as we should, and can. You have no one to watch right now. I have no chore to perform. So we start right this minute with a picnic at the

If you were in their place what would you do?

Jeanette...

Though she has survived a heart-wrenching tragedy, is there more unhappiness in store for Jeanette? She is hopelessly in love with a man who is inaccessible to her. Her story will come alive in the pages of "Beyond the Sweet Waters" by Anne Hampson.

Juliet...

Rather than let her father choose her husband, she ran...ran into the life of the haughty duke and his intriguing household on a Caribbean island. It's an intimate story that will stir you as you read "The Arrogant Duke" by Anne Mather.

Laurel...

There was no turning back for Laurel. She was playing out a charade with the arrogant plantation owner, and the stakes were "love". It's all part of a thrilling romantic adventure called "Teachers Must Learn" by Nerina Hilliard.

Fern...

She tried to escape to a new life...a new world...now she was faced with a loveless marriage of convenience. How long could she wait for the love she so strongly craved to come to her...Live with Fern...love with Fern...in the exciting "Cap Flamingo" by Violet Winspear.

Jeanette, Juliet, Laurel, Fern...these are some of the memorable people who come alive in the pages of Harlequin Romance novels. And now, without leaving your home, you can share their most intimate moments!

It's the easiest and most convenient way to get every one of the exciting Harlequin Romance novels! And now, with a home subscription plan you won't miss *any* of these true-to-life stories, and you don't even have to go out looking for them.

You pay nothing extra for this convenience, there are no additional charges ...and you don't even pay for postage!

Fill out and send us the handy coupon now, and we'll send you 4 exciting Harlequin Romance novels absolutely FREE!

A Home Subscription! It's the easiest and most convenient way to get every one of the exciting Harlequin Romance Novels!

...and you'll get 4 of them FREE

$5.^{00}$ GIFT TOKEN

Yes,

I'd like to take advantage of the Harlequin Reader Service offer.

Send no money get these

four books FREE

Mail this card today to:

Harlequin Reader Service
901 Fuhrmann Blvd., Buffalo, N.Y. 14203

YES, please start a *Harlequin Romance* home subscription in my name, and send me FREE and without obligation my 4 *Harlequin Romances*. If you do not hear from me after I have examined my 4 FREE books, please send me the 6 new *Harlequin Romances* each month as soon as they come off the presses. I understand that I will be billed only $1.25 per book (total $7.50). There are no shipping and handling nor any other hidden charges. There is no minimum number of books that I have to purchase. In fact, I can cancel this arrangement at any time. The first 4 books are mine to keep as a FREE gift, even if I do not buy any additional books.

CR952

NAME

ADDRESS

CITY   STATE   ZIP CODE

This offer expires Oct. 31, 1980. Prices subject to change without notice.
Offer not valid to present subscribers.

Get your
Harlequin Romance
Home Subscription NOW!

- Never miss a title! ● Get them first—
  straight from the presses! ● No additional
  costs for home delivery!
- These first 4 novels are yours—FREE!

**For exciting details,
see special offer inside.**

Printed in U.S.A.

BUSINESS REPLY MAIL

No postage necessary if mailed in the United States.

Postage will be paid by

**Harlequin Reader Service
901 Fuhrmann Blvd.
Buffalo, N.Y. 14203**

FIRST CLASS
PERMIT NO. 8907
Buffalo, N.Y.

creek. Ram will pack a hamper. Oh, and bring your togs.'

'My swimming things?'

'Why not?'

'There was a dog taken.' Polly told Gil about her first encounter with Thorn.

'He was very rough,' she remembered indignantly.

'Probably from concern. I would have been rough, too, but' ... an impudent grin ... 'for a different cause. But not to worry, we have enclosed baths. Only round the next bend, had you walked there. Just a fence, none of your mod, tiled, big blue bathtubs, but still good fun. I always thought so, anyway, and I know you will. In ten minutes, Polly.'

'Gil, I——' Polly did not know what she wanted to say. Although the reason for her job was away, she was still being employed, she was still being paid, and Thorn could resent this ... he probably would.

Gil did not wait for Polly to become vocal with her doubts. 'If you're not changed in ten minutes——' he warned, and gave her a loving push. Everything about Gil was loving and loveable, just as everything about his brother was not. Polly hesitated no longer, she smiled and complied.

When she came out to the verandah, Gil had a hamper and two large towels.

'Do you think,' he whispered as they set off together, 'that two people are watching us?'

'Two?'

'Thorn? Ainsley?'

'... Perhaps they are. It's hard to have to work when others play.'

'I suppose so.' Gil was silent a moment. Then he

hunched his shoulders. 'Don't let's brood on it, let's laugh.'

They did laugh.

They fooled around in the river baths until the tide receded and made water play impossible. Then they sat on the bank and ate Mrs Ramsay's lunch.

After the meal they lay drowsily in the sun until the first shadows encroached. Everything still stayed warm, though, and Gil's hand on Polly's bare shoulder was warm, too, but from himself, she knew, as well as the fading day. She gave a little shiver of pleasure.

'Cold?' Gil asked.

'Warm.'

He left his hand there.

Presently he said softly : 'Polly, you know that I'm sure about you, aren't you?'

Polly started to say : 'You can't be ... it's too soon ...' but stopped.

'I think I'm sure, too,' she whispered back.

Gil told her about this tree district, how once it had been parcelled under Lime Tree, then how the Clemances had sold the land up.

'Now there's a Fig Tree, a Cherry Tree——'

'An Apple Tree,' Polly nodded. 'I've heard of that one.'

'All very good for Clemance finance,' Gil sighed, 'but the money didn't bring my father luck. My mother died when I was very young. I can't remember her.'

'That's sad, Gil.'

'Yes. I would have liked to have known her, see if I took after her, for I certainly didn't take after the

Clemance side. Thorn did that.'

'What was Rollo Clemance?' put in Polly.

'My father's brother's son. His parents also died. He came to live with us, but I can't tell you much about him, I was packed off to school.'

'Your bad influence?' teased Polly.

'No, his. Rollo was the only agreement my brother Thorn and I ever had. We both hated him. Now enough of my skeletons, bring out yours. Thorn mentioned in passing, no doubt to try to put me off, that you were engaged to some English guy.'

'Yes—no. More a friendship thing.' How easy it was to say that now, thought Polly, when only a few months ago——

'You needn't excuse it, Polly, I don't mind. I prefer a girl with some experience behind her.'

That jarred a little, but Polly passed it over.

'I'll tell you if you like,' she proffered.

'Not a word. I told you I quite liked it. Besides, that was then, this is now. The burning question is what are we going to do with now?'

'I think we're doing a lot with now,' Polly smiled, making no attempt to escape from the arms he had placed around her. Why should she? she thought. She knew how Ainsley felt because Ainsley had told her, but that was then, and this, as Gil had just said, was now.

She listened to Gil planning for now.

'You're coming out with me tonight,' Gil told her as they went back to the house. 'Pink champagne, candlelight, the lot.'

'But Thorn——'

'Doesn't rule my private life as well as my working life. Does he rule yours?'

'No—no, of course not. But——'

'*Tonight*, Polly. We're going to celebrate.'

'Celebrate what?' she asked.

'Each other? Love?'

They were nearly home now, but oblivious of everything, Gil stopped and kissed Polly, and after a moment she kissed him back.

'Seven,' he said, and kissed her again.

Polly went quickly indoors, annoyed with herself that she had flashed Ainsley's office an unsure glance as she passed. All's fair in love, she found herself defending uneasily. I'm sorry for Ainsley, but oh, I'm glad for myself!

She ran a long hot bath. She took her time in dressing, selecting what she would wear. Gil liked gaiety, brightness, and she believed he would appreciate the glowing pink she finally chose.

She was standing by the window finishing her nails, watching the shadows edge out day, keeping an eye on the clock, when she heard the raised voices.

'You'll leave tomorrow, Gil.' It was Thorn, somewhere outside, probably on one of the long stone verandahs.

'I won't. I brought you back enough to keep you going for weeks.'

'Actually, and you know it, you brought back extremely little. Except trouble.'

'Trouble? Oh, you mean Polly? You don't like what's taking place?'

'Is something taking place?' asked Thorn coldly.

'What's it to do with you? You haven't a franchise on her as well, have you?'

'As well as what?'

'As well as whom, Thorn, and it was Serena I meant: Rollo's widow. What gives there, Thorn? Why are you keeping her out of circulation? What do you stand to gain?'

'I'll pass that—for the present. I have other things on my mind, and the main thing is I want you back on the job first thing in the morning.'

'You mean back on the job *here*?'

'On the road.'

'That's unfair!' protested Gil. 'You told me last time I might have a spell at Lime Tree, learn the basic principles.'

'Had you come back with what was expected of you I might have considered that. You didn't.'

'That's your reason, Thorn. Why don't you tell the truth? Why don't you admit you're frightened?'

'Frightened?' queried Thorn.

'Frightened and jealous over the fact that given any girl I can beat you to the post without even trying. You couldn't take a risk with Serena, the danger of losing whatever you stand to gain was too considerable, so you packed her off until I was safely away. Now you're resenting the fact that the girl you have staying here already, in only a few days, has——'

'That will be enough!'

'It won't be, though. Polly and I——'

'*That will be enough, Gil.*'

'It's not, and on the subject I must tell you a few facts, facts that you have to face. I can't help it if women prefer me. I can't help it if I can't be a sober-sides like the senior member of the firm. I can't help it if I have to kick over the traces. I'm Gil, not Thorn.'

'I'm well aware of that,' Thorn broke in, but Gil was not listening.

'Why,' he went on, 'even Ainsley thinks——'

'Remembering what Ainsley thinks is your first sensible remark.' Again Thorn broke in.

'I'm glad you said that,' Gil responded, 'because Ainsley, too, believes I should stay on.'

'You mean she realises the need for you to be continually watched.'

'You can go too far, Thorn,' said Gil angrily.

'You can go far too, Gil. You can go interstate tomorrow. Only tonight, my dear brother, *you're not going anywhere.*'

'You try to stop me!' shouted Gil.

Suddenly unable to listen any more, Polly shut the window. She looked at the clock. It was seven.

What was she to do? If she stayed here, Gil might come banging at the door, Thorn behind him, they might start another row. No, the best thing would be to keep the appointment at the garage as though nothing had happened, or at least if it had she had not heard it. Possibly, after what had taken place, Gil might not be there, but she had still better go, see for herself, then afterwards slip back into the house again.

Gathering her shawl and evening bag, Polly went quickly out of the room, down the hall and along to the garages. She saw that a car was out in readiness to leave, door open, the engine ticking.

She got in.

At once the car leapt forward ... typical of Gil, Polly thought, always in a hurry.

She had averted her glance when she had got into the car, not wanting to embarrass Gil, though he probably had no idea she had overheard, and probably, being Gil, he would not have been embarrassed.

Now, as they left the drive, she did look ... and caught her breath.

Thorn Clemance, not Gil, sat behind the wheel.

For a reckless moment Polly's fingers grabbed at her door handle. She did not turn it, though. On second, saner thoughts she withdrew the fingers again. Already the car had gained pace, and even if remaining here beside Thorn Clemance was the last thing she wanted, Polly did not seek an early death either. Though he must have sensed her change of mind, Thorn still took no risk. Without taking his attention from the unfolding road he leaned over Polly and checked the lock.

'I could still jump out at the first traffic light,' Polly reminded him.

'It would be useless trying, I've double locked the door so that only I can open it. To get out you'll have to climb over me first.'

'I could scream.'

'I doubt if you'd be heard. All the windows, except mine, are down and secured. Anyway, if someone was alerted I would say you were being hysterical. People shrink away from damsels indulging in hysteria.'

'Why are you doing this?' she asked curiously.

'You mean taking you out for the evening? Did you ask that of Gil?'

'He didn't take me,' Polly replied bitterly, 'you saw to that.'

'Yes,' he agreed coolly, 'I saw to that.'

'But why? *Why*?' Polly demanded.

'Why did I beat Gil to the punch? I considered it my right. As the senior brother I believed I should have the priority.'

'In what?'

For the briefest of moments he took his glance off the road. The look was enigmatical.

'I think,' he said almost in a lazy drawl, '*you* would have the answer to that.'

Polly fumbled furiously for words, but none came. She had never felt so enraged in all her life. At last she did find speech, and she asked him jerkily: 'Where are we going?'

'Where were you going with Gil?'

'He didn't say. He only said' ... a little remembering smile pushed through in spite of everything ... 'pink champagne, candlelight, the lot.'

'You have your answer, then,' Thorn Clemance shrugged.

'With you!'

'Why not? What did you expect? A pizza parlour? A street coffee stall?'

'If I did expect anything, and I did not, it would be much more dull and formal,' she retorted.

'Like I am?'

'You are, compared to——' Her voice trailed off.

'I take your point, Miss Kendall. I'm a dull, formal stick. And yet, if I dare remind you, there was a time when I was *not* so dull or formal.' Another quick look at her, and Polly felt her cheeks growing hot.

'However,' he went on, 'seeing you choose to for-

get, we must certainly remedy my dullness and for-
mality. Shall we try tonight?' He drove on in silence
and they reached the highway.

Once on the Great Western there was no opportunity for conversation, weaving a passage between
the busy night traffic took all Thorn Clemance's time
and skill. But presently he left the highway and followed a road to the left.

'Where are we going?' Polly asked again.

'To the moon. Even since its invasion I'm assured
it's still a romantic place.'

'Please make sense,' she begged.

'You mightn't like it if I did.'

'You're impossible!' she snapped.

'Not yet. But the evening is young.' He gave a low
laugh.

They had left the road now, and were travelling up
a tree-lined avenue. There were lights in the trees. At
the end of the avenue a large building rose up from
the darkness. Polly read a glittering sign: Montrose
House. She had heard of the Montrose; she supposed
most people had. It was not only a very select group
of restaurants, it was a sought-after and expensive
hotel.

'This is not just an eating place,' she objected.

'True, actually it's a number of eating places. I've
chosen the Flamingo Room for our night out. Tell me
afterwards if you approve of my choice.'

'It's a hotel,' Polly persisted.

'It is?' He pretended to look surprised.

'You know it is. Everyone does.'

'So?' was all his response.

'Gil was taking me to——'

'But was he?' A little edged smile now.

'I don't wish to go to a hotel!' she said angrily.

'Too late,' he shrugged. 'We're booked.'

'I don't wish it. Hotels have—they have——'

'They have accommodation,' he helped her. 'Is that what you're trying to say? Certainly they do, they provide suites as well as meals.'

'Mr Clemance, I——'

'Not now, afterwards. Here comes the porter to park the car, and I'm sure you wouldn't like him to think of you as naïve.' Thorn's smile flashed at her in the darkness of the car. He got out, came quickly round to Polly's side, unlocked the door and helped her out.

'How very beautiful you look tonight,' he said clearly for the porter's benefit, but his fingers under her elbow as he led her up the sweep of stairs to the vestibule were hard.

He had ordered a table by the window, and after they had been seated Polly sat looking out on the dark trees with their garlandings of lights.

'It's like Christmas,' she said, enchanted in spite of herself.

'Perhaps it is,' Thorn responded. 'I once read that Christmas was really a state of mind.'

'Merry Yule, jingle bells, Good King Wenceslas,' Polly mused. 'But I don't feel like that.'

'Yet you still saw Christmas,' he pointed out, 'so I think, in a way, you must feel it. Look' ... before Polly could voice a denial ... 'for a while, just a little while, let's play friends. I'd like to talk with you, Polly Kendall. It's something I've never done before.'

'Then what did we do before?'

'Attacked each other. Hated each other. Except' ... a pause ... 'on one occasion.'

She knew what he referred to, and she killed it at once. She said: 'We won't talk about that.'

'Very well then, but what? Art? Music? My long-forgotten youth? Your not-so-long? Name it and I'll participate.'

'You can't order a conversation like you can a dinner,' she persisted.

'Speaking of dinners, here is ours now. It looks good. See if you can come up with something equally good.'

'In conversation?'

He nodded.

'Then I can't.'

'Or won't. But thanks, anyway, for a starter. We'll make the subject: Can't or Won't ... Being unable to or refusing to. Now in my humble opinion——'

At first Polly would not co-operate, then the good drink, the good food, the good setting took over. She spoke to him; he answered her. Before she knew it she was laughing about something, forgetting to be bitter.

But it did not last long.

A silence crept in, and instinctively Polly knew that Thorn was going to break it in a manner she was not going to like. She felt herself stiffen.

Thorn refilled both their glasses, then he leaned across the table and said: 'It wouldn't have worked out, you know. I mean you and Gil, Polly. It wouldn't have worked even if Gil had intended to go on with it, and he didn't intend, he never does.'

'I think,' said Polly coldly, 'you're trying to tell me that Gil——'

'Not trying to tell you, but *telling* you. Any impression my brother might have given you as to his feelings for you would be entirely without foundation. It always is. Basically there's nothing there ... only for one.'

'Ainsley.'

'Yes.'

'Yet you told me before he was unaware of it.'

'I said he was deeply aware. But Gil *knows* all right.'

'Then if what you say is true why doesn't he——'

'Rush her as he tried to rush you? Because Ainsley is not so easy to pluck off the tree.'

There was a numbed silence now from Polly. At last she said: 'That was unpardonable.' She had gone a dull red.

'Yes, it was, and I apologise. I also should keep in mind my younger brother's quite exceptional charm, your own very vulnerable youth.'

'Thank you,' Polly said frigidly.

He shrugged, then continued with Ainsley's story.

'It was the old theme, Polly. Boy meets girl, they fall in love—the rest. Only this girl has upset the time-honoured progression. This girl won't accept the boy until the boy becomes the man.' A pause, then: 'Gil never has.'

'Ainsley could be wrong there,' Polly said eagerly, not feeling any hurt over what Thorn was telling her, but unaware of that fact.

'With Gil notching new conquests wherever he goes! Would *you* accept him, Polly?'

She did not answer that, she said: 'If Ainsley only

communicated with Gil ... let him know how she feels ...'

'You really mean add her name to the list.' Thorn paused. 'On the subject of lists, where did Gil come in yours?'

'I have no list, as you call it.' she assured him.

'Oh, come!' A low laugh. 'That fellow back in England. Probably many before him, for after all you're a very pretty girl. Then Gil.—Me.'

'You?'

'We were down a valley, remember.'

'... Oh, yes, I remember.' Her voice was tight.

'Then where do I come in?'

'Nowhere, and even if you did would I tell you when you tell me nothing? *Nothing*, Mr Clemance.' She looked at him and waited, knowing he must know what she meant, but there was no response.

She waited some moments longer, then she began fumbling for her bag and wrap.

'I don't want any more, thank you. It's been very nice, but I'm finished. Can we go home?'

'No,' he said, 'we can't.' He caught the waiter's eye and ordered more champagne.

'I don't want any,' Polly protested.

'I do.'

'You've had enough, you won't be fit to drive back.'

'I'm not driving back,' said Thorn Clemance. 'Not tonight.'

Polly sat very still. 'Then what,' she blurted, 'where——'

'This is a hotel, remember? You remarked on that yourself.'

'I know, and you're entitled to do what you like, but I'm going home.'

'You disappoint me. If it had been Gil——'

'It's not Gil, and even if it had been it would still have been home.'

'So you always come prepared with a return taxi fare?' he asked.

'No.'

'Meaning you haven't your fare now?'

'No.'

'Then how do you propose to get there? Walk? Hitch? No, don't clam up, tell me, I'm interested.' He had filled her glass in spite of her protests, filled his own. He toasted her. After that he gave another toast.

'To good hotels,' he said. 'Much better than walking.'

'All the same I'm walking out of this hotel in one minute, Mr Clemance.'

'Why the rush? Even if you flew back to Lime Tree you'd be too late—Gil would have left. I gave him his marching orders tonight.'

'I'm not going back to Gil, I'm going back because I don't want to stay with you. As for your marching orders, I heard them. I doubt if anyone at Lime Tree failed to hear.'

'So you knew when you came to the garage that it would be me, not Gil. Now that's interesting.' Thorn narrowed his green eyes on Polly.

'I didn't know. I went there because I'd told Gil I would. I pride myself on keeping promises.'

'All promises? Unspoken promises as well as spoken?'

'What do you mean?' she asked.

'Promises without words down in a valley?'

Goaded, Polly flung: 'I hate that valley! I hate you!'

'You disappoint me,' he drawled. 'When you turned up tonight after that unholy row I thought——'

'Perish that thought!' She went to rise.

A hand on her knee stopped her. 'We haven't had coffee yet.'

'I don't want coffee,' she said crossly.

'Then you can sit and watch me. Also I agree with you regarding the hotel, for frankly, under the present far from pleasant circumstances, I want to stop here as much as you do, but I do want coffee.'

'I don't. I'll go ahead.'

'Except that you're not going. I'm not handing you any money to be driven home, and I'm certainly not having you hitch.'

'Why not?' she challenged. 'Would it matter to you if something happened to me?'

'Of course it would. It would be awkward and time-wasting. I would have to attend court, say the last time I saw you alive. Now let me finish this, please.'

Polly watched him do so, wishing she had not been quite so hasty in refusing a cup. The champagne was bitter inside of her ... or was the bitterness because of him?

'Right,' he said at last, 'we'll go.'

He did not speak all the way back, and, taking her cue from him, Polly sat silent. When they reached Lime Tree she got out of the car on her own accord, and, leaving him to lock up, made her way towards the house. She was not aware that she was moving quickly until she heard his racing steps behind her.

The next moment he was whirling her round.

'Isn't it usual to thank one's host?' he asked her.

'Not usual for an unwilling guest,' she retorted.

'Nonetheless it's scarcely courteous.'

'I said thank you before, but if you want it a second time, then thank you.'

'Isn't it also manners to bid goodnight?'

'Yes, it is. I'm sorry. Goodnight.' She made as though to step away, but at once Thorn came forward and prevented her.

'Would you have said goodnight like that to Gil?' he asked thickly, 'or would you have said goodnight —like this?'

Before she could react, his lips were on her mouth, but it was entirely different from those other times. There was no preliminary to it, no experimentation, no prelude or lead up, just one hard, demanding kiss. In the fire and strength of it Polly knew intrinsically that she had never ever really been kissed before, not by Steven, not by anyone but this man.

She had shut her eyes, and when she opened them again it was to Thorn looking enigmatically down on her as he apparently waited for her to follow him into the house.

At the door of her room he said first: 'Thank you for your company' and then: 'Good evening.'

He waited till she went in and shut the door, then he proceeded to his own room further down the hall.

It was a long time after she had undressed and slipped between the sheets that Polly slept.

CHAPTER FIVE

POLLY always breakfasted on the verandah with Thorn, feeling it less trouble for Mrs Ramsay who additionally had Serena's tray to prepare since Serena never appeared for the first meal of the day. Apart from sparing the housekeeper, Polly had always been an early riser, but the morning after her dinner with Thorn, although she was wide awake Polly stayed in bed ... stayed, anyway, until she heard Thorn leave for his lab.

As she waited for his departure, Polly mulled over a variety of things. Thorn's show of propriety ... since Serena's absence Mrs Ramsay had been sleeping in the house ... so questionable in a male male like Thorn. Thorn's gross unfairness, demanding answers from her but offering her no explanation in return. Thorn's anger, never far from the surface. Thorn's——

Polly shut her eyes and determinedly switched from Thorn. Unfortunately she switched to herself, and at once she was sorry. She had been a fool, she thought, ruefully; she had let herself be manipulated by Gil.

She had meant nothing to Gil except a pleasant face and happy company, just as Gil's brother had implied. Worse still, and her first suspicion of it had come last night, Gil had meant nothing to her.

So why had she done it? How was she to face Ainsley?

At that moment she heard Thorn leave.

'There was a first-class row last night,' Mrs Ramsay gossiped busily when Polly came out later. 'Thorn told young Gil a thing or two, then he gave him his marching orders. He must have made it as though he meant it, because Gil left at once.'

'Wouldn't Thorn Clemance always mean it?' said Polly in a deceptively neutral voice.

'Yes, Thorn would,' agreed Mrs Ramsay cheerfully, 'but this time he must have made it much more forceful, because Gil got out quick smart, only leaving his usual note.' Now Mrs Ramsay sighed.

'Note?' For a moment Polly thought the note might be for her.

'He always leaves a letter for Ainsley,' went on the housekeeper. 'Gil never fails. I can't think why those two don't—well, why they don't—— Still, I expect it's nothing to do with me.'

A letter for Ainsley . . . Polly thought about this as she buttered her toast. She thought wryly, too, that this time yesterday she might have felt a pang of jealousy against Ainsley, a resentment against Gil. Not any longer, though, the brief enchantment, spell, spring madness, call it what you liked, was over, and all Polly felt was a fellow frustration with Mrs Ramsay that those two, Ainsley and Gil, that they didn't —didn't—— Polly smiled and shrugged.

After breakfast she drew a deep breath and went along to Ainsley's office.

Ainsley looked up at Polly in her usual calm way, then she smiled and waved her to a chair.

'Did you enjoy yourself last night?' she asked.

'I did not, Ainsley . . . but don't go thinking it was

because it was Thorn and not Gil who took me out, because you'd be wrong. I don't think I would have enjoyed myself with anyone.'

'Not in the mood? Yet you seemed happy enough when you came up from the baths yesterday afternoon,' Ainsley said carefully.

'You were watching?'

'Well—yes, I was.' Ainsley looked ashamed.

Polly smiled comfortingly. 'I had a feeling you were. Yes, Ainsley, I was happy, at least as happy as any girl can be with Gil.' She paused deliberately, intending to add: 'Except one girl.'

But Ainsley forestalled her. 'Only that happy?' she queried.

'Yes. Gil is charming; he's irresistible. I admit I found him both, but——'

'But?'

'But not for long.' Now it was Polly who looked ashamed of herself, of something that had been over almost as soon as it started. Deciding against long speeches, she asked: 'Forgive?'

'Forgiven.' But there was a sigh with Ainsley's forgiveness.

Polly picked it up, soft though it was, and sighed herself.

'I think it was because Gil was only ever half with me; I think he's only ever half with any girl he meets. The other half is with you.—Oh, Ainsley, why don't you realise that?'

'Someone's been talking to you,' Ainsley said calmly.

'Yes, Thorn did.'

'And what did Thorn say? No, don't tell me, I'll

tell you. He said that when it comes to girls——'

'That his brother only had feelings for one girl.' Polly did not add the insulting ... to her ... part about Ainsley not being so easy to pluck from a tree. Instead she added: 'You love him, you told me so once, so Ainsley, why? Why?'

'Why don't I tie him up, you mean? Because Gil is not ready ... yet.'

'You mean the man instead of the boy?'

'That would be Thorn again.' Ainsley's smile was wan.

'He'll never be ready if you don't make the move,' Polly insisted.

'I'm sorry, but I can't see it like that. I was brought up on man the pursuer, woman the pursued. It's a hard rule to break.'

'Ainsley, he wants you.'

'Just as he adds another notch to his belt,' Ainsley shrugged.

'Thorn said that, too,' recalled Polly.

'Oh, yes, Thorn knows his brother.'

'And has as much forgiving in him as you have.'

'Polly!'

'I mean that. I *mean* it, Ainsley. A woman who would only go halfway to the man she loves isn't worthy of him.' Polly began to warm to her subject.

'And how far would our speaker go?' It was Thorn who had come into Ainsley's office with a sheaf of papers under his arm. 'Fetch a butter box, Girl Friday,' he nodded to Ainsley, 'we're about to be harangued.'

'Not by me.' Polly closed her lips.

'Oh, come, you can't start something as intriguing as that and immediately drop it. Let us hear, and judge, the rest.'

'Some other time.' Polly had edged to the door.

He had put the papers quickly on Ainsley's desk and turned, but he was still too late to loom up at the door and stop her exit.

'I'll keep you to that, Miss Kendall,' he called to her retreating figure.

'Yes, do,' Polly retorted as she went out.

She wandered down to the bush track outside the home fence, the track where she first had met Gil, and the track, she smiled, where she had watched Serena and Rod Enderley walking arms entwined.

She wondered about Rod ... no need to wonder about Serena, she was in the care of her aunt and uncle ... how Rod had taken Serena's absence. She wondered if he was missing those meetings in the woods, for though Polly had only seen the pair once she had no doubt, by the familiar arms, that there had been previous occasions.

On a sudden impulse she decided to walk to Apple Tree where Rod had his practice. It was several miles, but it was a lovely morning, and after last night she felt she needed action, space ... and some male face other than that face of Thorn Clemance.

She knew the general direction, and set off through the bush until she reached the small road that meandered a charming, twisty way from Lime Tree to Apple Tree, to all the other Tree towns in this Tree district. It was a peaceful area, and Polly mentally applauded Rod Enderley's leisurely pace of medical livelihood until she saw the vast new housing venture that had taken place on the river flats. No wonder Rod had needed that mountain break away from his surgery.

She had no difficulty, once she reached Apple Tree, in finding the clinic. So far it was the only one in the small but promising town.

But when she went into the waiting room she did not find Rod. The doctor whom she glimpsed briefly every time a patient departed was younger than Rod Enderley.

At last it was Polly's turn. She went in and told the doctor apologetically that she was not here as a patient.

'That will be a change, anyway,' the young doctor said wearily. 'In Rod's shoes I, too, would have taken off.'

'Business too brisk?'

'You said it! Housing developments mean young families, and kids mean measles, chickenpox, mumps, the whole parcel. But sit down. You'd be one of the medical detailers.'

'No, I'm not, and I haven't any right here, really. I'm fine.'

'Fine, then.' The doctor was looking appreciatively at Polly's soft tow hair, wind-ruffled from her walk, her pink cheeks. He raised enquiring brows.

'I came to see Rod,' she explained.

'Good lord!'

'I beg your pardon?'

'*You* came to see Rod, yet Rod left to——'

'Yes?'

'He had business away,' said the doctor smoothly

and at once. He added: 'I'm locuming for him.'

'Yes, I can see that, but you said something about him leaving.'

'Did I? Oh, yes. It's this practice. Measles, chicken-pox, mumps, as I told you. You have to take regular breaks, especially when you're on your own.'

Polly nodded. 'I noticed this was the only surgery.'

'No, I didn't mean that, I meant the marital state —bachelorhood. A female can help a lot in a village practice, if only to sort——'

'The measles from the mumps,' Polly smiled and finished for him.

'Exactly. I'm thinking of buying into a village prac-tice myself, also with an up-and-coming child popula-tion, and my first acquisition would certainly be a wife.'

'A receptionist or a nurse would be less final.'

'But a wife more comfort.' He gave Polly a sly look. 'Any future plans?'

'I know nothing about reception work or nursing,' she shrugged.

'The other?'

'The comfort?'

'Yes.'

'I've just emerged from my last "plan", as you put it, a very unsuccessful one. No, thank you, Doctor.'

'I guessed as much. Well, I'm afraid that's all I can tell you. Rod simply rang and begged me to take over, and I'm here until he returns.'

'When will that be?' Polly asked.

'Why don't you forget him?' enticed the doctor. 'By the way, I'm Geoff Harris. And you?'

'Polly Kendall.'

'Of?'

'Lime Tree. You wouldn't know it. When will Rod be back?'

'When he comes, he said. You're sure about the other?'

'The wife bit?'

'Yes.'

Polly laughed and said she was sure.

'But you'll still take coffee? I hate drinking alone and I do need some.'

'Your patients——'

'Will only think you're having a detailed examination,' he grinned. He began pouring a strong brew into two mugs. 'Black or white?' he asked.

Half an hour later Polly left for Lime Tree again, once more through the woods. It had been an amusing interlude, which made her wonder why she was suddenly so absurdly apprehensive. There was no need at all to puzzle over such an unimportant and innocuous fact as Serena and Rod Enderley both being away at the same time. Rod, as his locum had reported, was merely renewing himself after an overdose of measles, chickenpox and mumps, and Serena was with her aunt and uncle, probably bored, possibly restless, but safe, secure and accounted for.

But a letter the next day told Polly that Serena was *not*.

The note was written in Serena's rather immature hand, and it informed Polly that she had left the relatives to stay a few days with some Queensland acquaintances. After that there was a line of surprise marks and a wicked: 'Which I have not, but Aunt are Uncle are pets and actually believed me.'

Polly read on and learned that Serena was staying at a Brisbane hotel. She would not be there long, so there was no need to tell Thorn. Naturally Thorn would still be thinking she was with the oldies, but really, Polly thought, although they were dears, they did fuss. Thank goodness they had proved easier to escape from than Thorn, though, and that for a few days she would be free.

Serena ended with: 'Don't worry, Polly, everything is going to be wonderful.'

It seemed rather an odd finish to Polly, especially that 'wonderful'—what was so wonderful about being alone in a hotel? Polly puzzled over it, but not enough to go to Thorn, something she sensed that Serena did *not* want.

Several more days went by, then at breakfast on the third day, Thorn present this time, he tossed across a letter to Polly.

'From Gil to you. Evidently he's chosen to do a Queensland stint, by the postmark. Well, aren't you going to open it and hear all about his big bad brother?'

No, Polly wasn't. She was looking aghast (but trying not to show it) at the name of Gil's hotel. It was the same as Serena's.

'Open it,' said Thorn thinly, 'I won't look over your shoulder.'

'I would consider reading any correspondence in front of anybody as rude,' refused Polly.

'All right then, I'll go. I was finished, anyway. Madam, will you excuse me?' He had risen by now, and he gave a mock bow.

As soon as he had gone, Polly opened the letter.

'Darling Polly,' Gil had written, 'the most remark-able thing has happened. Remember me telling you that I'd never met Cousin Rollo's widow Serena? Well, who did I run into yesterday in the hotel foyer but Mrs Rollo Clemance herself! I wouldn't have known if she hadn't been paged, but I would have wondered about such beauty. She's glorious, Polly. She's everything you said she was. I couldn't take my eyes off her. No wonder, I thought, my big brother is keeping her for himself.

'I've been trying to take her around, but for once in my previously charmed life I haven't found it easy'—Polly flushed at that—'Do you think old Thorn could have beaten me to it? She seems un-interested somehow ... imagine anyone uninterested in yours truly!'

There was more in the same half-laughing, half-boasting strain, and Polly scanned it quickly. Then she read all the letter through again. In the end it added up to one thing: Gil and Serena had met.

Now she supposed she would have to tell Thorn.

But before she could do any telling, Polly was to discover to her disgust that Thorn had some telling to do to her, and after it was over Polly changed her mind about any report to Mr Clemance. Already, she rankled, there were far too many words being tossed around.

It all began with Thorn's cursory summons to his lab. He rang through to the house, and Mrs Ramsay took the call. Polly, who happened to be in the kit-chen at the time, was only aware of Mrs Ramsay's: 'Yes ... yes ... I'll ask her now, she's right here.'

Before Polly could question the housekeeper, the

phone was down and Mrs Ramsay was telling her that Thorn wanted her over in the lab block.

Mrs Ramsay finished a little apologetically : 'He said to say at once.'

Itching with resentment at such an imperious message, Polly deliberately took her time in obeying. She washed her hands first, combed her hair, rubbed in some bright lipstick ... for courage, then slowly left the house and slowly crossed to the block where Thorn and Ainsley worked.

But if her steps were slow, Polly's heart was not. What had happened for Thorn to send for her like this? Had he found out about Gil? Had he discovered that his brother was staying at the same hotel as Serena? What was she to say when he taxed her with it, was she to tell him she had been about to tell him? Was she to——

She climbed the shallow stairs to the lab and knocked on the door.

Thorn did not bid her to come in, he opened the door himself and nodded to a chair. He also shut the door at once before she could have second thoughts, something she might have had, for he looked positively glowering.

She sat on the chair's edge, noting some letters on the desk and anticipating the worst. But when Thorn spoke it was on another tack altogether, though at first it did not sound like that.

'How long has this Apple Tree thing been going on?' he demanded.

'Apple Tree?'

'Your friendship with Doctor—Doctor——' Thorn hunted round his desk for a card. 'Doctor Harris.'

'I don't know a Doctor Harris.'

'Geoffrey Harris—evidently assisting at the Enderley surgery. Things must be looking up at Apple Tree.'

'Oh, yes, Geoff,' Polly recalled now.

'How long?' Thorn demanded.

'I don't understand you.'

'Then I certainly understood him.'

'Yes?'

'He called in today.' A pause. 'To see you.'

'Well, I didn't see him,' Polly insisted.

'No, you didn't.'

'But I was here. I haven't left the house once.'

'I was here, too, and I had no intention of letting you see him.'

'What?'

'Look, what you do outside my house and out of my employ is nothing to do with me, but while you are in my house and my employ, it has. I simply sent Harris packing.'

'You *what*?' she gasped.

'Packing. I ordered him out.'

'But——'

'It was like your nerve to go after him in the first place. Are you all that man-crazy that Gil hasn't gone a week before you have to fill a void?'

This was too much, even from Thorn Clemance, who always went too far. 'If I was, wouldn't I have tried you?' Polly's cheeks were crimson geraniums.

'I don't know, Miss Kendall. Would you?'

'Had I been what you said——' Polly began.

'I said man-crazy.'

'Then no. Not you. Not at all.' Polly added for

good measure, 'Never!'

'I'm answered,' he accepted drily.

'Can I go now?' she asked coldly.

'You can't. I didn't bring you over to discuss my effect, or non-effect, on you, I brought you over to be told what's taking place.'

'Taking place?' she queried.

'Between yourself and Doctor Harris. How does he fit in?'

'He fits into Rod Enderley's practice—Rod is away, and Doctor Harris is filling in for him.' The moment she said it, Polly was annoyed with herself. At once Thorn could question Serena's and Rod's absence at the same time, as she had, and it was bad enough to have Serena and Gil on one's plate.

But Thorn did not, he had other things on his mind.

'You still haven't answered me. Why did you go to Apple Tree in the first place? You knew I wanted the incident up at Blackheath closed.'

'As regarded Serena, yes. You made that very clear. But I'm not Serena and not your concern.'

'Under my roof you certainly are my concern,' he retorted.

'To be guarded, secured, dusted, then put back every day.'

He said grimly: 'There are other things I could think of, Miss Kendall.'

A little unsure of herself for all her indignation, Polly said as mildly as she could: 'It's all a storm in a teacup. I was simply at a loose end with nothing to do, so I took a stroll through the woods, found myself at Apple Tree, and decided to call on Rod.'

'But instead found Harris. How many meetings

have there been since?'

'None.'

He raised his brows steeply, and she knew he didn't believe her. 'Then today's would have made two?' he said narrowly.

'If I'd met him today.'

'Fair enough. Leave it at that.'

'If you mean don't see Doctor Harris, I'm quite agreeable, I never sought to see him in the first place. However, that might not stop him from trying to see me.'

'He won't be seeing you.' Thorn Clemance gave a quite devilish grin.

Polly was inflamed. Really, this man had gone too far!

'You can't rule me like you rule your cousin's wife,' she told him.

'My dead cousin's wife,' he corrected.

'Of course. And that makes a big difference, doesn't it?' She said it deliberately, but was totally unprepared for the quiet deliberation of his reply.

'Yes,' he said, 'it makes a world of difference.'

Polly had risen and now she stood there. Suddenly all the fight had gone out of her. The anger had fled. She hated this angry man . . . who wouldn't? . . . but no longer did he enrage her. All she knew instead was a deep . . . far too deep . . . hurt. Oh, she had been aware of his feelings for Serena, even down in the valley with his arms around her she had known them, but only in this minute did she realise what those feelings did to her. 'It makes a world of difference.' She heard his intense words again.—She *comprehended* them.

She turned and went a little stumblingly to the door.

He watched her go but made no attempt to detain her. When she turned to close the door behind her she saw that there were words on his lips, she could actually watch them forming there, she saw that he was trying to say something. Thorn Clemance unable to express himself!

She crossed to the house.

The domestic mail had been brought across, and Mrs Ramsay had put a letter from Gil in her room.

Polly opened it almost carelessly; she could not be worried about Gil being where Serena was any more. She could only think of what Thorn had said just now. 'My dead cousin's wife,' he had corrected. 'It makes a world of difference.'—*His* world? *Thorn's?*

At last Polly opened the letter and read.

'Dear Polly, If this surprises you, you can imagine how surprised I am myself. Gloriously surprised by a glorious girl called Serena. Yes, Polly, I've fallen in love with her. It's the real thing this time, I swear it. I know I must sound less than convincing, and especially to you, my most recent and very sweet love. But this time it's another story. Polly, I've really zoomed for that beautiful, wonderful girl.

'My head is bowed because of the hurt I feel I will inflict. To you, Polly? Thorn?'—No mention, Polly saw, of Ainsley.—'But I still can't change things. It's Serena all the way from this time on, and I wanted you to be the first to know.

'I haven't decided on any course yet. I did think of asking you to prepare a way, drop a few hints. But that could be dangerous with a man like Thorn.

Maybe you could tell Ainsley.'—So at last Gil mentioned Ainsley.—'No, on second thoughts, never A. Instead, tell nobody, at least until I stop spinning, until I catch my breath. Yours as ever, Gil.'

CHAPTER SIX

Now Polly waited every day for news from Serena. Gil had been in touch several ecstatic times concerning this 'new fresh sea' he was sailing ... (typical Gil words) ... but apart from that first communication telling Polly that she had left her relations to stay at a hotel, Serena had not written.

She must write some time, though, and Polly anticipated glad news sadly. For around Serena's and Gil's bright boat would be too many wreckages, she thought. The wreckage of Ainsley, who loved Gil, even though she would do nothing about it. The wreckage of Rod Enderley, who loved Serena. The flotsam of her own flimsy craft that had foundered almost as soon as it had been launched. Then Thorn's wreckage, for there was no doubt in Polly's mind that Thorn cared deeply for his dead cousin's beautiful wife.

So Polly waited, but no letter came.

It was now high summer, most extravagantly lovely of all Australian seasons, Polly considered. The uncertainty of spring over, the gardens were almost psychedelic with their sub-tropical flowers. The native trees, too, had shed their bark to stand new-minted and shiny, for here bark was discarded, not leaves as with the expatriates. An expatriate herself, Polly crossed to an imported maple to reach up and loyally touch its foliage.

'What was that for?' Thorn Clemance had come out to the verandah, and he stood looking down on her.

'It was because we're both un-belonging,' Polly told him. 'Oh, I know the maple is yours, duly planted and tended, but still in a way un-belonging.'

'As you are feeling now?'

'Perhaps.'

'Then I disagree. Admittedly you no longer belong to that fellow back in England, but' ... a pause ... 'belong here?'

Polly read a significance in his words, and gave a sigh intended to express boredom. 'So you're harping back to Rod Enderley's substitute again?' She gave a deliberate yawn.

'No, I'm not. Harris finished before he even began —I saw to that. Oh, no, Miss Kendall, there are other fish in the sea.'

'Then if the fish is your brother Gil, anything between us was so soon over it almost never began.'

'Good grief, you don't think I ever took you and Gil seriously, do you?'

'It certainly appeared that way,' Polly said resentfully. She was remembering the room that night, then the dinner afterwards at the hotel, scarcely her idea of fun. 'What other male had you in mind, then?' she flashed scornfully at Thorn.

'Me,' he said indolently.

'You?'

'There was, you may recall, an episode in a valley.'

'How can I forget it?' she pointed out to him.

'Then?'

'Then nothing, Mr Clemance.' There was no need

for Polly to lower her voice, since there was no one to hear. 'That episode, as you put it, was merely a diversion enacted by you until such time—I mean until——' Her words trailed off.

She soon saw that he was not going to let her get away so easily.

'Finish it,' he demanded.

'No.'

'I said finish it.' He had hopped down from the verandah and now he stood beside her. His hand shot forward and clasped Polly's, and the fingers were iron.

'I was a time-filler for you,' she said sulkily.

'I said *finish it*.'

'I have.'

'Oh, no, you have more poison in you than that, I think.'

'Then you think too much, and I don't need to finish anything.' Polly took the opportunity of a slight slackening of his imprisoning fingers to escape him. He did not try to detain her, he simply hunched his shoulders and proceeded across to his lab.

When he slammed the door definitely behind him, Polly felt a curious letdown. She did not like Thorn Clemance, she knew she never would, but that hard shutting of the door gave her a restless feeling she could not, and would not, credit. She had wanted him to go, hadn't she, so why was she like this?

It was boredom, she tried to tell herself. For all that she was a handful at times Serena was at least bright company. I suppose I'm missing her, she thought.

She considered a walk in the woods. Perhaps Rod

Enderley was back from wherever he had gone and might be walking, too. They could console each other. She could sympathise with Rod over Serena. Rod could talk to her about——

Polly gave a small start. About *whom*? There really had only been Steven, and Rod would never have heard of Steven. He would know as much, Polly mused wryly, as I know lately, for there had not been a letter from home for weeks. How were they progressing, that nice pair on whose account, and with Uncle Ben's prodding, she had stepped down? She had stepped down? She decided there and then to telephone home as soon as a chance to do so arose, the inactivity of the last week had unsettled her.

She would not do it when Thorn was around, though. She did not put Thorn Clemance above listening in. After all, he had done some sneaky things at other times. Like packing Gil off without an opportunity of speaking with her. Like seeing Rod's substitute before the man could see her.

Because of this, when a chance presented itself the next day, Polly promptly took it. Thorn and Ainsley had gone out earlier on what appeared, by their number of books, to be a long survey, Mrs Ramsay was in the middle of a big cooking project, the rest of the house and its environs so still it might have been asleep.

Polly decided on Ainsley's office as the safest from possible interruption. She closed the door behind her after she went in, then crossed to Ainsley's desk and took up the phone. She dialled the preliminary numbers, said what she required, and was told to hang up and wait. As she complied, Polly was only vaguely aware of a small noise from the direction of the door, almost as if a key was being turned in a lock. She glanced round and saw nothing there.

But at once there was a more definite interruption, this time the clear sound of a step beside her. Polly looked less idly now and was embarrassed to see Thorn standing there.

'You startled me,' she said.

'No doubt.' His lips were thinned. 'What are you doing here? Trying to steal my secrets?'

'If I was I would go to your office,' she said coldly.

'It's secured. I never take a risk.'

'Then——'

'But you could have gone there first, found you couldn't get in, then decided to try Ainsley.'

'What secrets would Ainsley have?'

'The ones she types for me.'

'Then I haven't stolen them,' she said. 'I came here because I wanted to telephone.'

'Why not use the house phone?'

'It was not a local call, and—and I thought I might be interrupted.'

Thorn said drily : 'Apple Tree is certainly local.'

'I wasn't ringing Apple Tree.'

'Well?'

At that moment the phone pealed, but Polly made no move to answer it.

'Your call?' he asked her.

'No, I don't think so.'

'Then answer it for Ainsley.'

'She mightn't like that.'

'She's not here to like or dislike it, is she?'

'No, but you're here.'

'Which you didn't expect,' he pointed out. 'I returned early to pick up some extra papers from the office. I was here when you came in and I heard you ring. Now, Miss Kendall, answer that phone.'

'I——'

'Answer it!'

Polly reddened. 'I assure you, Mr Clemance, that I intended to pay.'

'I assure you, Miss Kendall, you will. Now *answer*.' Thorn picked up the phone and fairly thrust it at her.

'Hullo?' Polly murmured miserably into the receiver. Then: 'Yes, thank you.' She wet her lips as the telephonist told her she could now proceed.

Like most overseas calls the connection came more crystal clear than any local one. Every word that Uncle Ben said could have been heard even in the next room. Polly knew Thorn must hear.

Uncle Ben greeted her affectionately, though reprovingly. Didn't she realise what time it was in England? Then he got down to answering what Polly had rung about, whether he wanted her home yet or not.

He did not.

'But soon, perhaps,' he cheered.

'Uncle Ben——'

'Steven is *not* missing you, Polly. You understand what I mean, girl.'

'But Uncle Ben——'

It was no use. Uncle Ben kept saying the same thing, and Polly kept protesting, or trying to protest, the same back. It all ended with some warning clicks, then Thorn Clemance leaning over and replacing the phone.

'After all,' he reminded her laconically as Polly looked angrily up at him, 'I'm paying.'

'I told you I would settle the bill,' she retorted.

'Until it's settled you're still in debt. Anyway, how long does it take to get an answer?'

'Get an answer?' she queried.

'As to whether you would be welcomed back, or not. Even as a disinterested listener it was very obvious to me that you were not wanted over there. Face facts, Miss Kendall, your would-be boy-friend does *not* want you. Not. N-o-t—a word of three letters. Can't you accept that?'

'Perhaps I could from anyone else, but not from you,' Polly said. She felt at the end of her tether.

'Then ring again.' He picked up the phone and handed it to her, still holding it out when she refused to accept it. 'Ring up and ask your Uncle Ben ... it was Uncle Ben, wasn't it? ... to do an encore.'

'You're incredible!' she gasped.

'So is your disbelief. You're spurned, Miss Kendall, not a nice thing to happen, I admit, but at least have the good sense and grace to accept it.'

'You have the wrong impression. You don't know what you're talking about.'

'I have a fair idea.' He dangled the phone before her. 'Come,' he said, and his eyes were more narrowed and more green than ever.

In a sudden rage Polly swept the phone from his hand, and the connection fell with a clatter to the floor.

'The telephone people,' he said laconically, 'won't be pleased about that.'

Polly did not answer. She left the phone where it

was and went to the door. Too late she recalled the click she had heard when she had been busy on her preliminary call. She realised now that he had locked the door and taken the key. She turned round to him in a silent request.

'Pick up the phone first,' he ordered her.

'No,' she muttered.

'Do as I say.'

'You shouldn't have said what you did.'

'Pick up that phone,' he insisted.

'No!'

'Polly, I was born an elder son, with an elder son's prerogatives, later I built myself a small kingdom of subjects, you could say.'

'Please go on,' Polly came in derisively, seeing his trend.

'I'm leading up to this: *I'm accustomed to being obeyed.*'

'Oh, I know that already. Don't forget I heard you ordering Gil out of the house.'

'Then?'

'No. Become *un*accustomed, Mr Clemance, and right now. Pick up the thing yourself.'

'You threw it,' he pointed out.

'You baited me.'

'Pick it up, or——'

'Or?' She was baiting him now.

'Or by heaven I'll make you, you completely maddening girl!' He took a step forward and put a hand on her shoulder.

She shook it off. 'Stop playing the big man,' she said scornfully.

'I am not playing—I am. If you have any doubt,

you stubborn little fool, do you want proof?'

Now he was a step closer, and though everything in her urged her to move, in that moment Polly found she could not.

Instead she stood silently waiting, knowing that he was going to take her in his arms, then when he did so she felt as she had never felt before with him. She felt suddenly awakened.

When he kissed her, she did not pull back, neither did she reproach him, remind him of diversions again, time-filling, say coldly that if this was his way of punishing her he was doing it well, for that was what she had planned.

Instead she stood tingling from his kiss, and when his hands explored the soft hollow of her throat, she knew an almost intolerable longing to react by testing the male roughness of his cheeks with her own cheeks.

When without warning he let her go again, and a weakness went over her, she looked up at him, trying to read what he was thinking.

But—— 'Pick it up,' he said. His face was expressionless.

Polly did.

He examined the phone for damage, then put it down. 'You're lucky.'

'I'm sorry. I shouldn't have done it. But——'

'But I baited you—you've said all that. All the same, I did.' A pause. 'So you can't leave here yet? Well, that suits me, because I have a job for you. To-morrow you're going up to Brisbane to accompany Serena home.'

'You—you've been in touch with her?' Polly saw

him give her a sharp look when she let out the guilty stammer.

'I suspect you know more than your oh-so-innocent face would like to express,' he said. 'I believe you're aware already that Serena is no longer where she should be, with her relations.'

'No—yes. But how did you find out? Did you ring them?'

'No, Serena wrote to me. The usual rot she writes, sweet, ineffectual. But she wasn't quite the clever girl she thought she was being. She mentioned her aunt and uncle, but she forgot one thing.'

'Yes?'

'Plain paper,' he shrugged, 'but a hotel envelope.'

Polly looked quickly at him, searching his face for a recognition, the recognition of the same hotel as his brother. But there was nothing there.

'She might have got it from her aunt,' she said a little foolishly. 'She might have finished her stationery supply and——'

'Only it didn't happen like that, and you and I know it. Serena had left the fold before she wrote to me, she was, and is, staying at this hotel. But not for long.' He gave a small smile. 'Tomorrow you fly up and fetch her home.'

'Mr Clemance,' Polly objected, 'Serena is an adult. Why, she's older than I am!'

'Making her not much more than a child,' he stated rudely. 'Anyway, enough of this, she's coming back, and you'll collect her.'

Polly said nothing.

'So now that you've obeyed me' ... a narrowed look ... 'will you kindly leave me to sign some papers

Ainsley tells me are very overdue. I intend to see to them now.'

Polly went to the door, remembered it was locked and turned back.

'The key,' she said.

Thorn was sitting in Ainsley's chair, and without looking up he tossed the key to her.

Polly caught it, took her time in opening up, in going out, in closing the door again behind her. She could not have said why she dallied ... why she half-waited ... she had had enough of him, enough for a lifetime, she thought, without spinning out time for more.

All the same Polly walked very slowly across to the house.

CHAPTER SEVEN

SERENA was at Brisbane Airport to meet Polly. Still with Thorn's instructions ringing in her ears, for the flight was not a long one, Polly walked into the big hall and was struck afresh by Serena's beauty. No wonder that Rod ... that Gil ... that *Thorn*——

'You can stay in Brisbane for a few days,' Thorn had told Polly, 'and then I want Serena back.'

Piqued at her own exclusion, Polly had said: 'But not me.'

He had ignored that. 'You can look around briefly up there ... I'm presuming you don't know Brisbane?'

'No.'

'Then look. After which——'

'Bring her back. I have the message.' Deliberately Polly had tacked on, as once before: 'Sir.'

He had given her that long green look of his, then had finished laconically: 'Have a good trip.' He had not waited to see the plane off.

Serena must have been shopping, the dress she wore was a new one, and very stunning. Polly said so as they made for the coffee shop and an exchange of chatter.

'Yes, it is lovely, isn't it. I chose it for my—I mean I wore it for——' But, typical of Serena, she changed to another channel.

'How is Thorn?' she asked.

'He's Thorn,' Polly said with feeling.

'And always will be. Still—dear Thorn.'

'Dear' Thorn. Polly stirred her coffee until some of it spilled over. 'Dear' sounded so pale, so thin, so inadequate for Thorn Clemance, so wanting compared to the deep passions she knew the man possessed for this lovely woman. He must possess them, she thought, otherwise would he have sent her up like this to bring her back?

'. . . Serena,' Polly said a little urgently.

'Yes?' Serena seemed surprised.

'You met Gil, didn't you? No, you can't deny it, because Gil wrote and told me.'

'Did he?' The violet eyes Serena turned on Polly were wide and seemingly innocent. She was, awarded Polly, rather surprised, a very clever girl.

'No, I'm not denying it, Polly,' Serena went on, 'I certainly met him. I met—others, too.' Now Serena's violet eyes fell to her hands, those slender white hands as lovely as the rest of Serena. For the first time Polly noticed a ring line showing faintly but unmistakably round Serena's fourth finger. She had always noted the other girl wore no wedding ring, but she had never noticed the evidence of a ring before. Then Polly saw the way Serena was looking at her hand, the absorbed way, and she bit her lip. Thorn had instructed 'Bring her back', but she knew he had not meant to bring Serena back with that dreamy look that she wore now.—Nor with a finger that showed evidence of a ring. Whose ring?

'Serena,' she heard herself demanding sharply, 'where's Gil?'

Again Serena gave her that wide-eyed look.

'I don't know. Should I?'

'Serena, don't try to put me off.'

'I'm not putting you off, Polly, I don't know where he is. Collecting specimens, I suppose. Even on his way home.'

'To Lime Tree?'

'He could be.'

'Without you!'

'Why should he take me back?' queried Serena.

'Because he fell in love with you. He wrote to me all about it. Also he gave you a ring. The evidence is still clearly there.'

At once Serena covered her left hand with her right. 'He didn't fall in love with me,' she replied, 'he only thought he did. I told him so from the start. Heaven knows' ... a sudden bitter pull to Serena's mouth ... 'I should know about love that's not love at all.'

It was the first time since she had known her that Serena had spoken like that, and for a while Polly was silenced.

'Gil told me he'd fallen in love with you,' she repeated presently. 'However' ... wryly ... 'I suppose I should know Gil by now.'

'Not you, too—' Serena was quiet a moment, then she laughed, and after a while Polly did, too.

'It was very brief,' she admitted.

'I think everything is brief with Gil ... except, perhaps, one girl?'

'Yes. Ainsley.'

'And Gil truly loves her?'

'I'm sure of that, only things haven't clicked.'

'But why, Polly?'

'Why don't a lot of things click? Why don't a lot of people behave as they should? *You* among them, Serena.'

'But what have I done?' asked Serena helplessly.

'I don't know.' Polly was looking down at Serena's covered left hand. 'Do you want to tell me?'

'I do ... yet I can't ... not yet. But I can tell you about Gil. Polly, he's nice, he's charming, he has everything, I suppose, but he was not, isn't, and never would be, for me.'

'... But someone else is?'

'Well——'

'And will be——'

'Well—Polly, we must leave it at that. You see, I promised.'

'Go on, Serena.'

'I made a promise.'

'Not to tell me?'

'Not to tell anyone.'

'And you're not breaking it?'

'No.'

'You sound serious,' Polly commented.

'Polly, I've never been more serious in all my life.'

'It it's not Gil, then——' But Serena was pouring more coffee, changing the subject, *closing* it. Her next trend was a world away. Polly could see it would be no use trying to probe her.

They remained in Brisbane for the rest of the day, but Polly knew that Serena's interest was only desultory, and that she was ready ... anxious ... to go back.

So they flew down the following morning.

As Thorn had not been told of the earlier return,

he was not at the Sydney terminal to meet them. Polly shrugged that it did not matter, it was not too long a journey for a taxi.

'There may be someone else from Lime Tree direction,' Serena answered ... and moments afterwards she said eagerly : 'Polly, there is. There's Doctor Rod.'

'How would Rod Enderley know to come?'

'Perhaps he had something to pick up,' Serena said vaguely, but there was nothing vague in the way she stepped out to greet the doctor.

Bemused, Polly found herself getting into Doctor Enderley's car beside Serena and driving through the city.

During the conversation on the way out Serena touched on the subject of Rod's substitute, and Polly gave her a quick look. Serena could not have known about any substitute unless she had been told, something she knew she had not done.

Someone else had given Serena a look, too. Rod had. The look silenced Serena's tongue ... but it did not stop Polly's thoughts. So those two have been corresponding, she deduced, Thorn would not like that ... *if he knew.*

But Thorn did not know, and Polly guessed that he would not be told either when he tackled Serena over dinner that night concerning her misdemeanours.

'Misdemeanours sound as though I'm still at school,' Serena tried to evade.

'I'm not being funny, Serena, I'm asking you a question. What did you tell your aunt and uncle, to escape like you did?'

'Only very little lies, Thorn, quite harmless ones. Aunt and Uncle were sweet, but—old.'

'You'll be old yourself one day,' he reminded her.

'Oh, I know, Thorn, I know, and that's why——'

'Yes, Serena?'

'Why—well, why I told a little lie and went away.' Serena half-glanced at Polly as if for help. 'Life is so short, Thorn,' she appealed.

'Are you sure that that's really what you were going to say just now?' Thorn asked closely.

'Of course.'

'What did you do all that time in the hotel?'

'It wasn't long,' Serena said evasively.

'What did you do?' he repeated.

'Brisbane is a very nice place, Thorn.'

'What did you do?'

'Bought things ... a dress.'

'But *do*?'

'I walked around,' she shrugged. 'The gardens are lovely.'

'*Do*, Serena. Do you hear me?'

'Thorn, don't shout!'

'I want to know. Serena, attend to me.'

'I am attending.'

'I've asked you a question. Answer it.'

'Thorn——'

'An answer, Serena.'

'Oh, for heaven's sake,' came in Polly, 'leave her alone!' The words had escaped her before she realised it. 'I mean, don't nag her like that. She's told you what she did. Isn't that enough?'

Thorn turned on Polly. 'Is it enough for you? Or perhaps you already know.'

'I don't know, but I would believe what Serena tells me.'

'Quite the believing little woman, in short,' he sneered.

'If you haven't belief you may as well give up.'

'Well, I haven't belief, but I'm not giving up. Serena, I want you to tell me——'

'Serena' ... it was Polly, and firmly ... 'you're only playing with your meal. Aren't you hungry?'

'I'm tired,' Serena said eagerly, eager to escape.

'Then go to bed, dear, and I'll bring some hot milk.'

'Stay where you are, Serena, I have a few more questions.' Thorn was at it again.

He had scarcely stopped speaking when the phone pealed. The three of them sat in the middle of its ringing, and only after a few moments did Thorn get up to attend to it.

At a signal from Polly, Serena escaped.

The call was evidently for Thorn, and it proved a lengthy one ... yet not long enough for Polly to escape as well. Anyway, at least she felt she should place the dishes in the machine.

She was doing this when Thorn finally put down the phone. He spoke to Polly from across the room.

'I employed you as company for Serena, not as an interference to me.'

'You were upsetting her,' she said defensively.

'I doubt it, but even if I were it was nothing to do with you.'

'I've become fond of Serena.'

'And what do you think I am, then?'

'I think you're *very* fond.' Polly gave him a moment to remark on this, but he said nothing. 'But I think, too, you're going the wrong way about it.'

'About what?'

'About fondness. *Very* fondness.'

'That's not good English,' he said banally.

'I wasn't talking about English,' she retorted.

'My God, neither was I! I was talking about Serena and the need to watch her until——'

'Until?'

'Until such time as——'

'As you're ready?'

'Yes, you could say that,' he shrugged.

'Then it's said, isn't it?' Polly switched on the machine.

'It's said,' he agreed coolly. 'Now get along with her hot toddy or whatever it is you promised her.'

'Milk.'

'Then come back here. I have a few things to say.'

'You mean a few more things.'

He did not answer, but he stood beside her as she heated the milk and poured it into a beaker. He was still there as she padded down the corridor to Serena's room.

When she reached the room, Serena was already asleep. Polly considered between waking her or leaving the beaker on the bedside table. In the end she decided to leave it, even though the contents would grow cold and form a skin. It was better than returning to the kitchen ... and returning to him. For already she had decided *not* to present herself, but to grab the opportunity and to go to bed as well. I will, she determined, even lock the door. She wanted no more probings tonight.

She silently and successfully crossed the passage,

then quietly opened, then closed the door, assiduously turned the key. Then, smiling a little, she switched on the light.

At once the smile faded. Sitting indolently on her bed, obviously amused at her careful performance, was Thorn Clemance.

'You're completely transparent, Miss Kendall,' he drawled. 'I knew you'd do this.'

Polly stared incredulously at Thorn. She could not believe that any man, even a Thorn Clemance, would have the blatant audacity to come into her personal room like this, especially with Serena's room only a short distance across the hall.

Thorn looked levelly back at her, then he rose from her bed, pushed deliberately past her and removed the key from the lock.

He slipped the key in his pocket.

'Well, Miss Kendall?' he drawled.

'You ... you ...' Polly began furiously. Then, and compulsively, she stopped.

For now his level look was losing its indolent amusement and an entirely different expression taking its place. To her utter dismay Polly felt her own anger receding, something else stealing in. She recognised it because she had known this feeling before. It had been down a valley ... that hateful valley ... this man had stepped across to her down there, put his arms around her, and then ... and then ...

Now Polly tried to force herself to stiffen. She must became incensed again, she thought. With resentment gone, resistance could be gone, and she had to resist Thorn Clemance. I was, and I am, only a diversion, she reminded herself forcefully. Simply a means of marking time until such time as——

'I want to talk to you,' Thorn was saying.

'Then I have nothing to say to you,' Polly returned, 'except——'

'Except?'

'Why are you here?' She glanced significantly around them.

'I told you—I want to talk to you.'

'No,' she refused.

'Yes, Polly. We're going to talk. Now.'

'Later.'

'Now.'

'Then if you must, it has to be outside,' Polly ruled.

'In the garden? Oh no, you'd only escape me there.'

'The lounge, then. Your study. But definitely not here in my room.'

'Why?'

She looked at him in irritation. 'Isn't it obvious?'

He looked back with thin amusement. 'A regular Miss Grundy. I didn't know you were so prudish.'

'Aren't you something of a Grundy yourself? A chaperone every time there are only two in the house!'

'I agree with you there, and similarly regret it.'

'I didn't say regret.'

'I did. However, it had to be like that because of Serena.'

... Serena, Serena, would it ever stop?

'A pattern had been set,' Thorn went on. 'I could scarcely go to Chaperone Ramsay and tell her to move in whenever Serena was here but out whenever you were.' He smiled obliquely at Polly.

Polly ignored the smile. 'Why should you have to do either?' she asked.

'Serena is an answer that I'm not ready to give you yet, and I think' ... the oblique look again ... 'you already have that second reply.'

'Have I? Then I don't know it. The only thing I do know is that your prudishness is quite ridiculous, quite incredible, in a man like you.'

'And what kind of man is that?'

'A—a male male,' Polly stammered, wishing now she hadn't started it, 'a full measures man.'

'I see. Well, I find your objection not to talk here equally ridiculous and incredible in a female female and a full measures woman. For you are that, Miss Kendall.' Unlike Polly, he did not hesitate with his words. He waited a moment, then demanded: 'Why are these four walls so different from the rest of the house?'

'I'm not debating differences, I'm simply saying that anything you wish to tell me must be told outside.'

'Inside. Here. In spite of my household arrangements with Mrs Ramsay, I'm not a prude, and we are not leaving here. After all, I own the house, so I call the tune.'

'As always,' Polly said bitterly.

'You think so? It seems to me that if I have it's been a very inaudible tune; also I haven't called it of late.' His green eyes were narrowing now on her.

Instinctively Polly glanced to the door again, but she remembered he had removed the key, so there was no hope of making a dash for it.

'Why are you afraid?' He had followed her look,

and he was regarding her with indolent amusement
once more.

'I'm not.'

'People who run are always afraid,' he drawled.

'I haven't run.'

'Only because you know you can't get away.' He
had taken the key from his pocket, and he spun it
lazily between his long fingers. 'I want a reckoning,
Polly,' he said.

'A reckoning?'

'An understanding. An undertaking. I'm sick of not
knowing where you're going. I have to be told.'

She looked at him with amazement. Where *she*
was going? What right had he to ask that of her, he
who never confided anything? She started to tell him
so, tell him bitterly, then all at once her words were
trailing off, and instead she stood looking at him
while he looked quietly back.

There was silence for a long, long moment, a
silence you could almost *feel*, thought Polly. She
knew that a subtle change was taking place.

She had averted her glance before this, but secretly
she darted him another look. His unanswering stare
in return completely disarmed her. It was not just an
estimation, a regard any more, it was something
more actual, almost, she sensed, like a gentle stroke
of his hand. The sweetness instead of challenge
caught her completely unprepared, and Polly
flinched.

'You're afraid,' he interpreted at once.

'Afraid?'

'To give me what I asked: a reckoning, an understanding. You're afraid of what it could start.' He

paused. 'Now. In this room.'

Deliberately she ignored that last. Instead she echoed him : 'Afraid of what it could start ?'

'In both of us.'

'You're ridiculous—it could start nothing.'

'I'm not so sure,' he taunted. 'Oh, I'm certain of my own reaction, have no two thoughts about that. But I'm not sure of your sureness, Polly, your so-called sureness of yourself. I keep on remembering—a valley. I will admit that after the valley episode I had an icicle on my hands, but down there——'

'Will you please stop!' Polly's voice was a little hysterical.

'You're denying it ?' he demanded.

'No, I'm despising it.'

'Despising it ?' He looked at her sharply.

'Yes.'

'Then either you're a liar now or you were a very good actor then.' His green eyes were narrowed and his smile was reminding.

'And you're not a good actor, Polly Kendall,' he went on, 'so you must be lying. It was as important to you that morning as it was to me.'

'Important!' Polly near-shouted it, and Thorn stepped forward at once to stifle the sound.

Immediately Polly stepped back, forgetting that behind her was the locked door. She felt the knob burrowing into her back, and instinctively, although he still had not quite advanced, she put up an arresting arm as though to ward him off. To her dismay she realised she had misjudged the distance between them, and instead of waving him away her hand was now positioned across his chest.

He wore no jacket, no singlet, only a thin transparent T-shirt that followed the hard muscular lines of his body. He moved slightly ... deliberately or unintentionally Polly did not know ... and she found that now her hand had slid from its first position and was resting instead directly across his heart. The heart was beating strongly, and it gave her a sudden unbidden feeling of strange excitement. The deep strength of the beat seemed to mean—it could mean—— Oh, you utter fool, Polly Kendall, it was only a normal throb, and even if it wasn't, you do not like this man, remember.

... No, not like, perhaps, but—love him? Could there be no liking yet still be—love? Polly hadn't thought so and she told herself fiercely that she could never wish so, but one thing was becoming very certain in this moment: that while still disliking she still loved Thorn Clemance.

He had put his own hand up and had cupped it over Polly's hand still resting across his heart. 'Listen,' he invited. 'Hear it.' Then he said: 'Feel it.'

'No.'

'Then I'll feel yours.'

'No!'

For reply he took his hand away from her, but only to pull her to him. When she was close enough his lips closed down on hers.

The strength that had been receding from her ever since she had come into the room and looked at him was now at a very low ebb. Resist, she thought feebly; he's only playing with you again, playing as he always plays, he's filling in time, he's—— But instead, weakly, she clung.

She did not fight him even when he sank back on the bed again and pulled her with him. She did not edge back when he began kissing her again and again.

His hands touching her were not the strong hard hands she always knew as his but suddenly feather-light and exquisitely tender on her quivering skin. The feel was virtually a caress.

He now had his head buried in her breast, and he was saying things she could not follow because of his muffled voice, but she sensed every word ... and one word she did hear. 'Need', she received clearly. 'I need you.' At once the rosy mist that was whirling around her began to disperse. Of course he had need of her, the way nature had arranged it man had need of woman, but in Thorn Clemance's case since the woman he really wanted was not available yet, then the need had to be satisfied somewhere else.

Polly began saying things back to him, things she knew he could no more hear from her than she had heard from him. But he must, as she had, have sensed the meaning.

She kept talking, and as soon as she could move from the weight of him now heavy against her she pushed him away. Ordinarily she would not have had a chance of moving him, but all at once he had risen up from her, and raising his hand he slapped her lightly, so lightly it was barely even a brush, across one cheek.

'Thank you for nothing, Miss Kendall,' he said frozenly, and he turned away from her.

Polly sat up less quickly. She did not know exactly what she had said to him, probably a continuation of her bitter thoughts, but the brush of his fingers had shocked her. Not the actual contact, that had been nothing, but the act itself. He had slapped her. This man had slapped her!

He was putting the key in the lock now, turning it. When the door opened, he threw the key violently back at her.

'Now you can lock yourself in,' he said. Then he added: 'Though there's no need for you to lock yourself from me. Now or ever.'

He went out.

Polly did go over and turn the lock, but had she examined her action she would have realised that she had only moved automatically, that she had no fear of any return from Thorn. What had he said? 'Now or ever.'

She came back and sat on her bed and stared at the closed door. Now or ever. She repeated it quietly aloud, tasted it ... then bit down on a trembling lip.

An almost paralysing cold began creeping over her, and she sat still and pinched and numb.

Presently she ran the bath in the adjoining en suite, and when she stepped into the hot water she lay long and motionless in the warmth but still feeling chilled and numb. As the temperature of the water dropped she added more heat, but she still felt cold.

She must have stayed there over half an hour, just staring ahead of her, not even stirring enough to cause a ripple in the surface, hearing the house noises one seems to hear at night, the sigh of a little wind disturbing a window blind, the stir of a curtain, the slur of a branch against a wall, the creak of furniture.

And the front door being opened and being shut again.

That noise, anyway, was actual. Polly got out of the bath and cuddled herself into a thick towel.

She put out the light. Already the light was out in her bedroom. In the darkness she crept to the bedroom window and peered outside, she had previously noted that one of the windows had a particularly good view of the exterior of the house ... especially the garages. For it was to the garage that Polly felt Thorn Clemance was going now. She knew it would be Thorn, there was no one else to leave the place save Serena, and that quiet but strong shutting of the door certainly had been distinctly male. She watched until her eyes ached through watching, then she saw the garage door that housed Thorn's car being opened, and then for a moment, in a flicker of moonlight, Thorn himself. He went into the garage, and presently she heard an engine ticking. Soon afterwards the car shot out much quicker and more recklessly than Thorn ever drove it. Letting off steam, Polly thought derisively, driving for miles to get something out of his hair. Driving for miles. She repeated those three words several times. Driving for miles. But miles took time, and in that time——

Only waiting for the car to clear the avenue, she turned back, then lit up the room again. Then she went to the wardrobe and took out some bags. Quickly, carefully, she began to pack.

Even as she selected, folded and arranged, she could not have said what she intended doing. She only knew she had to get away, that life under the same roof as Thorn Clemance had become intolerable, that if she saw him again and told him what she was intending she could not be responsible for what else she might say or do. She only knew she simply had to leave, and that now was an opportunity she might not get again.

Miles take hours. Again she found herself thinking about that. Thorn had left in a flaming temper, a temper that would take its time to level out again. Obviously he had left in his car to spin through the night, lose himself in darkness, drive and drive until his unreasoning was lost and his reasoning regained. Then and then only, she supposed, would he come back. In that time——

Now Polly's brain was thinking coolly and progressively. She would not take her own car, it would be too conclusive. Thorn could return to the garages, notice its absence and possibly set out after her, start everything again. But with the car still there he would naturally believe she was in bed. He would not come and knock on the door to make sure. He had, and Polly smiled bitterly, had enough of her for the night. For all nights?

She would take only necessary things. The rest could stay here. She could send for them later, she shrugged, but it really didn't matter. She had only brought one bag and an overnighter from England and had not accumulated much. Now she discarded the bag and instead crammed the overnighter. It would be easier to handle. She was careful to put in her passport, her papers and money, though even as she did so she still had no plans.

She paused a moment at Serena's room, longing to go in and bid a silent farewell to the girl, for she had grown extremely fond of Serena. But although she had little doubt that Serena would have slept through any goodbye, she still decided not to take any risk. Instead she put her fingers to her mouth, then moved in the direction of the sleeper. After that, as Thorn had, she went down the hall, then opened and shut the door.

Now she went carefully. Her theory of Thorn driving angrily through the night might be only idle conjecture; already he might be on the way back. In which case she must literally creep along, skirt the drive, hide behind any concealing trees ... slink. Polly leapt triumphantly on that word. She would slink.

She did. She literally crept until she reached the road that led to the highway, and even then she kept close to the bushy rim.

But nothing came along, neither on the drive nor on the road, and some time later she gained the Great Western Highway.

Now she went even more warily. A glance at her watch told her that all that had happened tonight had taken its toll of time, and that dawn should not be far off. But it was still dark, that dense, eerie dark before light, and she did not fancy a car coming suddenly to a halt to pick her up.

It did not happen, though. Polly walked so close to the bordering fences that only a spotlight would have disclosed her, and presently the first fading occurred, soon afterwards a primrose glow, and finally a buttery sun. The night was over. Morning had come.

Polly reached a bus stop and sat in the shelter. She had no idea of any timetable, whether it was a regular bus that ran, and if it did come where it would go.

She did not know how long afterwards a bus did

lumber up. It was an early workers' bus, and no one took any notice of Polly as she climbed in. She tendered some coins and the driver said: 'Station?' to which Polly nodded.

When she got to the railway she went with the others to the side of the platform that seemed more in demand at this time of day, and when the train arrived, she, too, got in. As they left similar stations behind them, Polly realised by the closer settlement that she had done a right thing, that she was travelling towards Sydney, not going further west as unknowingly she might have. Sydney, she thought confidently, she knew sufficiently well by now.

When she reached Central, Polly made at once for the airlines office where she still held a return voucher. Her mind was clear at last, she had come to a decision, and her steps were certain.

She took her receipt to the desk, and after some checking and a period of waiting, the clerk told her he could get her on a cancelled noon flight to Heathrow.

It was really only then that Polly actually realised that she was leaving everything behind her. That welcome or not, and who could know for sure with an Uncle Ben? she was going back to England. That she was turning a page of her life, her Australian page. That she was closing a chapter called Thorn Clemance.

CHAPTER EIGHT

To form a new friendship on her long flight to England would have been the last thing Polly would have asked. Had she been given a choice she would have shrunk from sitting beside a stranger who fast became less than a stranger, from liking the young man placed beside her enough to respond at once to his eager conversation, most of all to enjoy a journey she had not expected to enjoy, had only thought of as a dreary return.

When she had been shown to her seat Polly had planned only on sitting back, closing her eyes, letting the hours, miles and clouds spin by her ... trying to think.

She did all of these, but most important she found no time to think. Instead in an incredibly short time she was sharing a drink with Kerry Waldron, sharing a movie, sharing meals, laughter, conversation, sharing ... as far as one of them was concerned ... a slice of life.

It was Kerry's life that was revealed. Polly remained quiet over hers. But Kerry, refreshingly naïve, disarmingly friendly, did not seem to resent her reticence.

'This is my first trip,' he told Polly, 'and the name is Kerry Waldron. I've been lucky enough to sign up several firms back in Sydney, each allowing me a small retainer. No great fortune, but enough, when added together, to look after my basic wants plus a little over. I'll have to go carefully, though, and that's where you'll come in.'

The magazine that Polly had hoped to hide behind had dropped to her lap. 'Me?' she asked.

'Yes, you. You're English, aren't you? I heard you thank the hostess. So you'll have to help.'

His choice of words amused Polly. They were the authoritative words that Thorn Clemance would have used, she thought, only never, *never*, in this impetuous, boyish manner.

'Have to, Mr Waldron?' she queried.

'Kerry. And I'm sorry. But you know what I mean. You are——?'

'Polly. Yes, I know what you mean,' Polly said musingly. The authority, unintentional in Kerry's case, would have been very intentional in Thorn's. She was silent a vexed moment. When was she going to stop recalling that man? She turned with deliberate charm on Kerry, anxious to put her past behind her, and he was delighted with her favour.

'What comes after Polly?' he asked.

'Kendall. Now tell me about your venture.'

With alacrity Kerry did.

He had finished his story with an urgent appeal to Polly as to where she thought he should dig in once they reached London.

'I was not a city girl, Kerry, I lived in the country,' she told him, 'Well, more rural, anyway, than you had in mind.'

'And you're going back to this rural village?' His disappointment was unmistakable.

She thought that over for a few moments. 'Perhaps not yet,' she said.

'Then?'

'I'll see how jobs go. I had a council job before, but it would be filled now. Besides, I don't want to go home, not for a while.'

'Then, Polly?'

'Then?'

'What will you do?'

'Do? I'll try my luck in London, I suppose.'

'Meaning you'll live in London?'

'... Well—— Oh, really, Kerry, you do probe!'

'But I have to probe,' he pointed out. 'This, as I said, is my first bid to success. It's obvious I must live centrally, but when you don't know where central is, what do you do?'

'Don't look at me, Kerry, I told you I'm a country girl.'

'But an English one. If you're not going home where are *you* digging in?'

'It would be of no interest to you,' she discouraged.

'But it would. I could tag along, be advised as to whether the digs I got were at the right place, the right price. You could help.'

'Kerry, grow up!' she scolded. 'Young people, ones younger than you, arrive in London every day and find their own way about.'

'But only because they have no one to advise them like I have.'

'Have you?'

'Yes.' A grin. 'Polly.'

He was immature but winningly so. When he preposterously suggested later that they save costs by sharing a flat, Polly had to laugh.

'But you must agree that a single bed-sit can be a very expensive and quite depressing fate,' Kerry argued.

'I do agree, but it's still no.'

'Two can live cheaper,' Kerry reminded her next.

'Perhaps, but not this two.'

He took the refusal cheerfully. He was an amiable boy, Polly thought. He said with mock reproach that he was confident he would meet up with someone who would be glad to share, and then Polly would be sorry.

'Meanwhile,' he finished, 'here are the addresses of my London contacts.' He handed them to her, then while she studied them, he dozed off.

Polly made pencilled notes on a piece of paper, trying to decide which London or near-London base would suit Kerry best ... which would suit her best as well, until such time as she returned home.

She had worked out previously that she had several clear weeks ahead of her. There never had been any regular correspondence between herself and the family. Her sister had only written when Polly had written. Uncle Ben had written only when he had a request. Steven had not written at all. No one would be alarmed if there was no Australian mail for some time, or if their letters, if they wrote, were not answered promptly. As for Lime Tree, as she had left behind most of her clothes and her old car, Thorn Clemance would naturally think she would be calling back, so would do nothing. Yes, Polly thought, as she pencilled busily, she should be quite safe.—Safe, too, she mused, if she shared a flat with this Kerry

Waldron now asleep beside her, not like she would have been with—— There she went again!

Determinedly she put down her pencil and closed her eyes, too.

The pair of them drifted the rest of the way to Heathrow.

An early morning arrival left them the whole day to reconnoitre. By ten o'clock Polly was leading Kerry around a handy district that it had occurred to her would be most suitable for both of them.

Rents were higher than they used to be, she found, but she assured Kerry that a *single* bed-sit should not horrify him too much.

'Look, Miss Grundy,' Kerry retorted, his boyish grin taking away any of the offence that Thorn Clemance had intended when he had called her that, 'I don't want that kind of bed-sit.'

'But Kerry——'

'You read my impressive list of contacts, Polly,' Kerry reminded her. 'How could I proudly bring a client home for coffee to a room with a day-bed and a gas-ring?'

'You entertain out, Mr Waldron.'

'I still think——'

'And the answer is still no,' Polly laughed.

Kerry thought it over for a while, then shrugged good-humouredly.

'I think I'll take over after lunch,' he proposed. 'You're doing well, Polly, but not well enough.'

'Do better, smarty.'

'Oh, I will.'

Kerry left Polly soon afterwards to return almost at once.

'I've got it,' he said triumphantly.

'You can't have.'

'An entrance hall, balcony, mod cons, the lot.'

'Also,' deduced Polly, 'from that description two bedrooms at least.'

'I thought that was what you would insist on, Polly.' Kerry looked innocent.

'You're incorrigible! *I* am not insisting on anything.'

'Suit yourself, but it's the only accommodation offering, and the agent said the three of us could move in at once.'

'Three?' she queried.

'I thought that might interest you,' Kerry grinned. 'It's quite a large flat with room enough for three or even four, but I thought we'd keep it at two and a chaperone for our Miss Grundy.'—Miss Grundy again. Thorn Clemance once more came flashing into Polly's mind.

'One bedroom for you,' Kerry went on, 'one for the new guy and yours truly. With a shared rent it should suit all our pockets. Well, what do you say, Polly?'

Polly said laughingly: 'I suppose under the circumstances, yes,' and Kerry beamed from ear to ear.

'The third tenant is called Smith,' he told Polly. 'Peter Smith. His firm took the agent's message and said that Peter would be delighted. We're all to meet at Home Sweet Home, for it is that, in an hour.'

'Then we'd better leave at once,' Polly said urgently, 'I want to pick my bedroom.'

'It will be the one with the single bed,' Kerry advised, 'unless——' He gave Polly another of his impudent looks.

'No,' Polly smiled again.

Kerry complained unconvincingly: 'Don't you ever answer anything but that?'

It proved a pleasant apartment—airy, light, on the top floor of three levels. Polly liked it at once.

She was examining the bathroom when she heard the bell ring, then Kerry go to the door. Instead of voices there was silence, and, intrigued, Polly went out.

A girl was standing in the small entrance hall staring uncertainly at Kerry. Kerry was staring back and seeming a little stunned. It could be the girl's looks, Polly decided, she was certainly very pretty, but at that juncture Kerry found words, and it wasn't the girl's appearance, it was the fact that she was a girl. He said so.

'But I thought you would be female,' the girl retorted. 'Kerry?'

'Kerry was originally a man's name. I took you to be a man. Peter?'

'With an A, not an ER.'

They both laughed.

'Anyway, it will still solve Miss Grundy's conscience,' introduced Kerry of Polly.

'Kendall, not Grundy,' Polly said, 'and I'm glad you're coming, Peta.'

'Am I coming?'

'Look, let's sort it out over coffee. The previous tenant has left a few sprinkles of instant coffee and I've found three mugs.'

Over the brew, milkless, without sugar, Polly said:

'There's only one thing that worries me, Kerry. What, when you bring your big clients home and they find us girls here, will those VIPs think?'

'Think? They'll envy me my harem,' Kerry gloated.

It was settled at once.

Not only did Peta supply a third, she soon supplied a job for Polly. The firm where she worked needed a receptionist, and within a week Polly was almost as settled as if she had never left England.—But only almost.

She missed Serena. She could not have credited that she could wish so sincerely she could see that lovely, unpredictable scatterbrain again, but she did. She missed Ainsley, missed her steady eyes and her gentle voice. She missed Gil, impetuous, quite impossible Gil. She even missed Mrs Ramsay, and she certainly missed her cooking.

... But Polly always stopped her missing list at that.

She did a lot of wondering, however. In the morning while Peta slept in the other twin bed, Polly would lie wondering.

She wondered if a conclusion had been reached to that far-off story yet, that Lime Tree theme as she called it to herself. Had Finis been written at last? Had Thorn Clemance fulfilled his self-imposed waiting period and claimed Serena Clemance? Had Rod's heart been given the blow she believed it could have? Had Gil been desolated over his unsuccessful meeting with his cousin's widow? How badly had he reacted? Or had he, characteristically, recovered at once? Had Ainsley stopped being the Ainsley she set herself out to be and done what Polly had advised? Had——

'You're pensive, Polly.' It was Peta, awake now, but yawning.

The girls, by mutual scheming, had got into the habit of waiting for Kerry to bring in early tea, a chore he continually complained about but still performed.

There was a silence, then:

'I came away in a hurry,' Polly proffered uncertainly and inconclusively.

'From Australia?'

'Yes.'

'And now you're wondering what's happening over there since you left?' Peta was intuitive.

'Well—in a way.'

'Can't you write and ask?'

'No, Peta, I can't.' The two girls were on close terms by now and always spoke honestly with each other.

'... That way, is it?' Peta said shrewdly.

'No—no, of course it's not,' Polly said at once, and was not surprised when Peta just smiled. She was a very perceptive person.

'Methinks the lady doth protest too much,' Peta suggested.

'Then you think nonsense.'

'Do I? Ah, here's tea at last.'

'I don't like that "at last",' Kerry protested as he came in with a tray. 'I'd be careful if I were you, young Peta, or you might find yourself doing the job!'

'While you do what?' Peta grinned, holding out her hand.

'While I sit back in comfort waiting to be served as you are.'

'That will be the day,' teased Peta.

'*Will* it?' Suddenly Kerry's voice was very serious, and Polly felt that her own presence made one too many in the room. She had sensed this often of late. There was no doubt that Peta and Kerry had clicked right from the beginning, that every day things between them were getting deeper.

Polly had even decided to move out, to leave that nice young pair to plan what they wanted from life without her. She had mentioned it to Peta, and Peta had said: 'Yes, Polly, we guessed you were intending that, but don't go yet, please. You see—well, we want to be absolutely sure.' A confident smile. 'We don't think we'll keep you waiting long. Meanwhile promise us to stay on just as you're staying now.'

'You mean a third in the house?'

'Well, at least not a lone girl in a single bed-sit. Will you promise?'

Polly had promised ... a promise she was to be conscious of a week later as she crossed the street from the shop on the opposite side to the flat.

A man was standing in front of the flat, and he very obviously was waiting for her.

Polly stared at him quite foolishly, forgetting the fact that she should not have been so surprised to see him when he had always worked here. He had commuted every day from the village, and now his presence explained to Polly why this particular corner of London had instinctively been the first place to occur to her when Kerry had needed his base. Unfamiliar with any others, automatically she had chosen this.

Vaguely thinking this, she stepped forward as the man stepped forward. 'Polly!' He came right up to her with both arms outstretched.

'Steven!' Polly returned.

Steven was the first to start talking. He jerked his head towards the unit block and asked: 'Aren't you going to invite me in, Polly?'

Polly hesitated, not knowing what to do. Peta was away for the day, only Kerry was present, and for no real reason Polly felt suddenly awkward about introducing the two men.

She saw that Steven was watching her closely, and she flushed, making the situation even worse. She wished she could be sensible, and explain, but somehow she couldn't, all she could think to say was a stammered: 'I can't invite you in, Steven. Not at the moment. You see ... well ...'

'It's all right, Polly.' Steven patted her arm, something he had done often, Polly recalled, a friendly gesture, but she, little fool that she had been, had taken it seriously. A song to sing to, and Steven had been her song, or at least she had thought so.

'I know how it is, Polly,' Steven was telling her. 'You see—well, I've spotted him before. I' ... a little apologetically ... 'saw him go up your stairs.'

'You sound,' Polly tried to banter, 'as though you've been spying on me!'

'Yes, it does sound like that, but I wasn't. I saw you across the street one day, but I wasn't quite certain. I mean, you were supposed to be in Australia, so I decided it couldn't be you. The next day I saw a man go into the same flat, and I told myself I'd been wrong.'

'Then the next day again you saw me a second time and knew you hadn't been wrong?'

Steven nodded.

'And now,' Polly shrugged, 'you're thinking that Kerry and I—that we——'

'Why shouldn't you?' interrupted Steven strongly. 'I wouldn't have liked you to be cloistered up living on a memory.'

'That's nice of you, Steven, but you really should have said living on a wishful thought that I never should have allowed, anyhow. You never had it.'

'No, Polly dear, I didn't, you were just a very nice, very companionable little girl to me.'

'I know, I know. Uncle Ben told me.'

'Uncle Ben.' Peter sighed. 'Polly, where can we talk? We do need to talk—you know that.'

'There's a coffee shop round the corner,' Polly said.

'Lead on!'

They did not speak again until they had reached the small shop and found a secluded table in the corner.

'Why did you sigh when you said Uncle Ben?' Polly asked anxiously. 'Isn't he well?'

'He's fighting fit for over seventy,' Steven assured her, 'and the sigh was because through being well-meaning ... too well-meaning ... everything that should have happened didn't happen.' Now Steven shrugged.

'You mean you and Lucia didn't——'

'I mean that, Polly. We didn't start our happy ever aftering as soon as we should have had you simply stayed on. Why did you do it, you silly girl? Why did you go away? But don't tell me—I know. Uncle Ben.'

Polly nodded. 'He said it was the only way.'

'It was the only way *not* to bring us together,' Steven told her. 'Instead of hurrying things, it sadly delayed them. Lucia immediately thought the obvious, that you'd left because you couldn't bear to stay. Your sister wouldn't make one move, nor let me make one, until she knew how you *really* were.'

'I wrote,' Polly pointed out.

'Letters.' Steven shrugged again.

'But I was over it, Steven. Not for a while, I admit, but afterwards. I am now. I doubt really if I was ever into it. You were only, as Uncle Ben said at the time, a song to sing to. When I got away, well——'

'You forgot the tune?' This time Steven grinned.

'Something like that,' Polly smiled back.

The waitress brought coffee and Polly took a long sip before she spoke again.

'You told me just now that you didn't start your happy ever aftering as soon as you should have. Does that mean' ... she smiled hopefully at Steven ... 'that you have now?'

'Yes, we have now. It happened definitely when——'

'Yes? Yes? Go on, Steven.'

But Steven didn't. He sat silent for quite a long time, and Polly had to encourage, 'Go on, Steven,' again.

'Well—I don't know if I can after all, Polly,' Steven said unhappily. 'I just don't know.'

'Don't know what?'

'Nothing—nothing. Polly——'

'Yes, Steven?'

'Polly, do you love that fellow?'

'What fellow?'

'The one you're living with? Look, I'm not being big brotherish—heaven forbid! It's just—just——'

'Just what, Steven?'

'Polly, I'm confused,' he sighed.

'Then your confusion is nothing to my confusion. Just what are you talking about, Steven?'

But Steven would not, or could not, say.

They parted outside the coffee shop. Yes, Polly said, she would come down soon. She looked hard at Steven, trying to probe him, read, delve, unearth. But it was no good.

She went slowly back to the flat.

Polly postponed her going home for that week. Something had happened, and Peta needed every moment of Polly's support. After all, as Peta announced gladly, you don't get married every day.

Polly expressed no great surprise, she had known it was coming, but she *was* unprepared for Peta's busyness, and said so. Why the feverish packing when it was Peta and Kerry who were uniting and stopping on, and she, herself, as the third, who was moving out?

'But we're not staying here, Polly,' Peta told her. 'Kerry's contracts are finished, successfully finished, and he's going back to Australia.'

'And you with him?'

'Whither you go, I go,' said Peta contentedly. She

added: 'I only wish——'

'You could take your family, too?' Polly broke in sympathetically.

'I have no family. No, I was going to say I only wish you were coming.'

'But this is my home, Peta.' Polly said it routinely, though, feeling nothing in her at all.

Peta and Kerry were married the day Kerry finished his last duty. After the ceremony they flew straight out. It was as quick as that. They were both apologetic about leaving Polly the big apartment, but Polly brushed the thought aside. She would either get a bed-sit, or she might, if another job was offering, go back to the village. She felt she could now that the happy ever aftering was progressing favourably. She laughed as she told the departing newlyweds this, but there was a little hidden doubt in her. It had happened when Steven had said unhappily: 'Do you love that man you're living with? I'm not being big brotherish. It's just——'

Just *what*? What had Steven *not* said? All he had admitted to was that he was confused.

Again Polly thought: No, *I* am.

She came back from Heathrow to the unit. She would look around at once for something smaller and cheaper, she could not afford to stay on here.

She climbed the stair flights very slowly. She felt oddly flat ... she felt unwanted.

At the top of the landing she burrowed for her key in her big bag. The wretched thing eluded her so that she did not see the figure that had positioned itself between her and the door.

When she looked up at last, she caught her breath.

She had been surprised by Steven, yet she still had known that she must see Steven at some time. But she had not known she would see ... she never had expected——

Thorn.

CHAPTER NINE

CASUALLY, as though appearing unannounced twelve thousand miles from home was a daily occurrence for him, Thorn Clemance removed the key from Polly's suddenly lifeless fingers. At once, at the touch of his fingers, Polly's own fingers felt blood tingling in them again. She jerked her hand away, but now that he had the key he did not seem interested enough to stop her. Instead he stepped around her and placed the key in the lock. He turned it and opened the door. After that he nodded Polly inside. In all this time he had not spoken, but when Polly still stood he asked tersely: 'Or do you prefer to be carried?'

Now Polly found words, too. She retorted: 'A bride's prerogative, surely.'

'Which you are not. Not' ... his green eyes narrowing ... 'that you haven't tried, Miss Kendall.'

Polly turned on him sharply. 'What do you mean?'

He had preceded her inside, and he waited until she came in, too, before he spoke.

'Shall we start with Steven Marchant?' he suggested. 'I have no knowledge of any of the candidates before him.'

'Nor any knowledge of Steven,' she told him furiously.

'Correction: I have met, and I approve of, Marchant. I commended your taste at once. Next came my brother Gil. Then that doctor fellow. Note, please, that I'm not putting myself on the list. Now' ... looking around him ... 'there's this apartment.'

'What's wrong with this apartment?' she demanded.

'Nothing, of course ... except that it is scarcely a spinster's secluded setting, is it?'

'You took pains to tell me once,' Polly dared, 'that one room and four walls were enough when one was in love.'

'Meaning you aren't that? Not in love? Hence two rooms and eight walls? Yet are the two rooms needed?' He was crossing arrogantly and flinging open the doors to first Kerry's, and then Peta's and her, rooms. At the two beds in the second, unmistakably feminine room he was silenced a moment, but, characteristically, not for long.

'Guests?' he enquired blandly.

'No, another tenant. There are—were—three of us. Two females, one male. Satisfied?'

'Not yet. There's a lot more to be cleared up.'

'Not by me.'

'By you,' he said. He took up a chair, carried it across to her, then firmly pressed her into it. He brought another chair and put it directly in front of her, not more than a foot away. There was only a small distance between their two pairs of eyes.

He waited a deliberate moment, then he said: 'Steven Marchant reluctantly reported to me that you were living with some man.'

'Reluctantly?' Polly asked.

'It was the last thing he wanted to report. He knew it could ruin everything for himself and Lucia. For nine months he'd been getting nowhere with your too-sensitive sister, then when at last ... through me ... he thought he might break through, this had to happen.' Thorn spread his hands and looked around.

'I don't know what you're talking about,' said Polly, 'and nothing has happened.'

'I have to be convinced of that, but first of all in all fairness I must tell you all I know.'

'I don't want to hear.'

'All the same you're going to. Now keep quiet.'

He waited until Polly obeyed, then he resumed.

'It seems you have a unique sister, Miss Kendall, one who couldn't bring herself to build her own happiness on your unhappiness.'

'I wasn't unhappy,' Polly protested.

'They ... Lucia and Steven ... didn't know that until I came on the scene.'

'How could they know it then?'

'Simply because I told them. I told them I loved you, that you loved me. That I'd come over here to marry you. Everything was rosy after that until——'

'Until,' broke in Polly a little shrilly, not for a moment permitting herself to think about what this man had just said, 'by chance Steven saw me.'

'Exactly. At first, aware how Lucia's and his future depended on your future, Steven was overjoyed.'

'And then,' continued Polly, 'he saw Kerry going into the same flat the next day, put two and two together according to him, and was promptly disillusioned.' She sighed. 'I know it all.'

'No, not quite all. You see, when Steven unhappily told me, he no doubt expected that I would consequently bow out, go home again, that nothing would eventuate. Learning from honest Steven that you'd forgotten me so promptly that you'd already picked up with someone else should have desolated me as it did him, Steven thought, for Steven *was* desolated, Polly, he could see another long period of waiting while your sister fretted over the fact that she'd ruined your young life.' A short, wry laugh. 'Only I happen to be stubborn, as you know, and I did not bow out. Instead I got this address from Steven, and here I am now.'

'Oh, I can see that,' Polly said in a trembling voice, for she was finding it hard to keep her control. After a moment she asked : 'But how? How are you here? How did you know where to find Steven to ask him? How did you know I would come back at all?'

'It was easy,' he said unashamedly. 'I opened your letters. But even before that I knew you'd be somewhere in England. Not for a moment did you fool me with your subterfuges, Polly. Leaving behind you a car, a wardrobe of clothes, was too, *too* obvious. I saw at once that you were only pretending you'd be returning for them. I knew you wouldn't.'

'All right then, you spied and discovered where my home was, flew over, then went down there,' accepted Polly, 'but why? Why?'

'To find you, of course.'

'To make me account to you for an unfilled contract?' Polly asked a little wildly, for she still refused to believe those things he had said.

'No, you little fool, there never was a contract.'

'Then?'

'To finish what I started, Polly. This.'

He had got up from his chair, and as he rose he

pulled her with him. He held her away from him for a long, deliberate moment, his green eyes no longer those considering slits of his but wide open this time, looking at her, looking fully, almost devouring her, drinking her, if eyes could, then he closed her to him, and the lips that crushed on to her lips blocked out everything, the room, the doors leading from the room, the apartment, everything disappeared in one kiss.

'I love you.' Polly heard it distinctly yet distantly. 'I loved you from the first moment I saw you making shark bait of yourself down the river. If you can remember, I even told you so that day. I said that up till now my work had comprised my entire life.'

'But I thought you meant Serena.'

'You thought too many things,' he retorted.

'Previously,' he resumed, 'I'd learned something about you from your ex-boss. Foxton had told me a little of your history, the fact that you were recently "displaced", as it were, presumably not in the right state yet to love me as already I loved you. Yes, Polly, I mean that. Bells rang for me down the river that day. The whole universe exploded. But I knew I had to wait.

'The wasting days made me—well, restive, I suppose, impatient, on edge. Already I had Serena on my hands, and the fact that I couldn't have you, and the comfort and help of your love while I saw Serena through, maddened me. I suppose I was sometimes—heavy-handed?' He looked enquiringly at her.

'Heavy-handed?' she echoed. 'You were an angry brute!'

'Yes, and I realised you must be feeling that about me, and I did try ... believe me ... to soften up. I tried often. But you would never listen, never respond, never encourage me. You fought all the way. Why?'

'Because of Serena,' Polly said clearly, briefly and stonily in reply.

'Serena? But we had all that out long ago. You actually thought she was my wife, didn't you, when she was my——'

'She was your cousin's widow,' Polly nodded. Then she added: 'But—your love?'

'My what? Oh, you idiot of a girl! I loved, and do love, Serena to the ends of the earth. Who couldn't love that lovely, helpless thing? But I never cared for her. *Care*. Do you understand that word?'

'Then why——'

'Why did I do what I did? But I thought that would be obvious. She had to be protected—surely you could see that?'

'I could see she wasn't quite ready for things yet, I sensed that she'd had some unfortunate experience, but I didn't know what it was.'

'So you interpreted my love and protection of Serena as reserving her until such time as it would be considered "decent" to claim her for myself? Is that it?'

'Yes,' said Polly.

'But good grief, woman, you could never seriously have thought that?'

'I did.'

'But look at me. *Look*. Do I seem the type to you

to wait, for whatever reason you care to concoct, for something I want? Do I?'

'It did seem foreign in you,' she admitted.

'Foreign!' He pulled his arms away from her. 'Foreign! Had I wanted Serena I would have gone ahead, inheritance or not, I wouldn't have waited one minute more.'

'Inheritance?' Polly stared at Thorn, her mouth dropping. She was remembering Gil discussing his older brother one day, wondering about Thorn's close care of Serena, then suggesting that perhaps Serena was well-heeled and finishing contemptuously with the statement that every man, however rich, wants more.

But if that had been the case, why was Thorn here now, why was Serena over in Australia?

'I don't follow you,' she said in a stifled voice.

'I thought you would,' he said with disappointment. 'I thought you would understand instinctively, not need it all to be spelt out.'

'I don't understand, and it does need spelling. Thorn' ... sharply ... 'I mean that.'

He looked at her ruefully. 'There are many other things that I'd sooner do right now than explain, but I expect you should know. I suppose in my over-care of Serena I did forget to tell you a few things.'

'Over-care is the right word,' Polly sighed, 'and you did forget.'

'Very well then, we're going to clear this up now.'

He pushed her down on her chair again, then sat down himself. He looked steadily across at her.

'Rollo Clemance was not my cousin,' he began.

'But you said ... Gil said ...'

'There was no need for Gil to know, so we never told him.'

'We?' she queried.

'My father and I. I'm a lot older than Gil, as you know. There was no need for Gil to be told either that our mother had *not* died very early, but instead had left to live with someone else.

'The result of the break-up was Rollo, only a year after Gil. When the fatal accident happened and our mother and the man for whom she had left our father were victims, Rollo was taken in by Dad ... but as a cousin. It sounded better that way.

'I never took to Rollo. He's dead, and we're taught we shouldn't speak ill of the dead, but I could never speak well of him.'

'What about Gil?' she asked.

'Was nearer his age, and nearer his temperament in many ways, but no, Gil didn't like him, either.

'Rollo was a smug, self-satisfied boy. All right, most of us are, but even as a child he had a cruel streak. When he was young he practised it on anything or anybody he came in contact with. When he was older he used it on his wife.'

'Serena?'

'Yes.'

'Serena never spoke of him,' mused Polly. 'I often wondered why.'

'Serena couldn't have brought herself to *think* of him even. He was that kind of man.

'Serena was an orphan. Her aunt and uncle had put her through boarding school. I don't know how Rollo met her, but he plucked her out of her last college year at some ridiculous age and married her.'

'But if he was like you say he was why did she agree?'

'She was immature, still is; probably she was flattered, probably she was bored with school, not exactly jumping for joy at the prospect of a life with nice but dull relations. Also, Rollo was very good-looking in a flabby, flashy, self-indulged way, and he moved in a smart circle.'

'He fell in love with her?'

'Never Rollo, the only person he ever loved was Rollo. But she was young, she was exceptionally beautiful, she was a feather in his cap, something to show around.

'I expect he duly showed her; Seréna has always been as reticent about him to me as she was to you. But at once he discarded her.'

'He left her?' Polly was shocked.

'No such luck. I don't know what he did to her, Polly, I daren't think, I only know that when I saw her at Rollo's funeral I was distressed beyond words.'

'When was all this, Thorn?'

'Two years ago.'

'Two years?' she gasped.

'It's taken all that time to repair what's been done to her, to bring her to the frail state she is now.'

'Two years ... you mean you only recently brought her to Lime Tree?'

'From the sanatorium,' he nodded. 'With her aunt's and uncle's assent I'd placed her there.' He rose now, paced the room, came back again.

'When my father had taken Rollo into the family, he had made him an equal member the same as Gil and me. That was characteristic of my father. He didn't restrict it just to education, he catered equally financially for him, too. The only difference was that the business was for his sons only, Rollo could not come into that. But rather than lose, Rollo gained ... or at least he would have had he not died. Ironically, through my father's skill, the sum my father invested for him skyrocketed. He stood to reap more than Gil and I ever would. But he died before he could.'

'Leaving Serena a very rich widow?'

'Not at once. You see, Rollo predeceased my father, leaving his wife only a very moderate amount. My father at once changed his will to benefit Serena instead ... but with a stipulation.'

'Yes, Thorn?' Polly said.

'As I told you, the effect of our mother's unfaithfulness hit our father terribly. He had worshipped her.'

'So much so that he took in her son,' Polly nodded.

Thorn agreed. 'But the bitterness,' he added, 'was still there, and when it came to settling Serena, Father drove a very hard bargain. With the preservation of marriage in his mind ... it was an ever-present factor to him, almost an obsession ... Serena had to remain Rollo's widow for a stipulated period at least.'

'You mean not remarry until then?'

'Yes. Otherwise the large sum that Father had built up for Rollo was not to pass to his widow. I suppose you're thinking that that was harsh of him, but he'd been treated intolerably, remember, and the hurt had never left him. Besides, he was really protecting Serena. Although many men would have married her for her loveliness, many more would have married her for gain.

'Perhaps if Dad had met Serena, realised her simpleness, he might have constructed something else, but he never saw her, for he died soon afterwards, and what could I do when I was left with my father's last wishes? You see, Polly, I was his executor as regards Rollo's side of the legacy.'

'And did you execute!' came in Polly accusingly. 'You banished Doctor Enderley.'

'Did I?' Thorn gave a maddening smile. 'Oh, no, all I did was see that Serena did nothing reckless.'

'Like marrying again too soon?'

'Yes.'

'Your brother tried,' she remarked.

'Of course Gil would try. Gil always tries. Undoubtedly he tried, too, with you.'

'But you saw to that.'

Thorn hunched his shoulders, but kept smiling.

'However,' he admitted, 'Rod Enderley was more of a problem. Even without you telling me I suppose eventually I would have seen and accepted him as something different.'

'Someone *special*,' nodded Polly, 'only you had to spoil it all.'

'Did I?' Thorn asked again.

Polly waited for him to elaborate, but he did not go on, and presently, tired of his smiling silence, she said: 'So that's the end of the story.'

'The end? It's only the beginning, Polly. My brother and Ainsley are married. No, don't look so surprised. You can't be, seeing that you organised it.'

'I?' she queried.

'You told Ainsley to change her methods, remember? To go the whole way, not just halfway, to the man she loved. Well, Ainsley did just that. Now she's Gil's wife, and I've lost a perfect Girl Friday.'

Polly waited, for she knew there was more to come.

'The day Serena's inheritance, according to my father's decree, was due, I stood myself down,' said Thorn.

'How did you do that?'

'I told Serena everything, then warned her that she was on her own from then on.' A small laugh. 'Do you know what that minx answered? She said "Not on my own, Rod and I were married three weeks ago in Brisbane. We've been waiting to tell you, but you haven't given us a chance." '

'That's believable,' broke in Polly feelingly. Before he could answer, she asked: 'Was their marriage before or after the date?'

Thorn hunched his big shoulders. 'It didn't matter. It never would have mattered.'

'But your father——'

'He'd loved our mother enough to take in Rollo. Even after everything he had still had love. So don't you agree, in spite of words written down, that he really would *not* have bothered about that?'

'But you and Gil——' Polly reminded him.

'We have enough.' Thorn looked deeply at her. 'Our coffers are overflowing,' he said.

There was silence for a while. Thorn broke it. He mused: 'Serena's and Rod's marriage made two marriages. It must be the season. Yet things go in threes.—Do *you* know of any impending third?' He waited for her reply.

'I know of a certain third, not an impending one,' Polly answered. 'The two, Kerry and Peta, whom I've just seen off at Heathrow, were married before they left.' She paused. 'Kerry was the man' ... challengingly ... 'who shared this flat.'

'And Peta beat you to the punch?'

'You're a brute ... as always,' she complained.

There was another silence, and then:

'Only because you look for brutishness in me,' Thorn said, 'only because you never look for tenderness. Please look for it now, Polly Kendall, *look for it*, for it's there. It's there for you.'

He was pulling her gently to him, and his touch was incredibly, unbelievably soft.

'You're a tune in me,' he said, 'that keeps on spilling its notes.'

Polly looked at him in surprise. 'Uncle Ben once said that I was young, so had a song to sing,' she told him, 'and that what I interpreted as falling in love was really only a singer looking for a song.'

'Was that true? Or was Steven your song? Gil? Doctor Harris? Kerry? Someone else you sang to?'

Now his big arms were enfolding her quietly, with infinite care and yet with a firmness Polly could never mistake, and she knew there would be no half measures with Thorn Clemance, no half way but all the way with this man.

But Polly also knew with a soaring certainty that no one had been her song, but that Thorn would be.

She looked up and told Thorn so, and he threatened : 'It had better stop that way, Polly Clemance, or——'

But he was kissing her as he warned her, and Polly heard her heart beginning its song.

Whoever said, she smiled to herself, that this was an angry man?

4
FREE
Harlequin Romances

TAKE THESE 4 FREE

Harlequin Romances

as advertised on TV

Thrill to romantic, aristocratic Istanbul, and the tender love story of a girl who built a barrier around her emotions in ANNE HAMPSON's "Beyond the Sweet Waters" . . . a Caribbean island is the scene setting for love and conflict in ANNE MATHER's "The Arrogant Duke" . . . exciting, sun-drenched California is the locale for romance and deception in VIOLET WINSPEAR's "Cap Flamingo" . . . and an island near the coast of East Africa spells drama and romance for the heroine in NERINA HILLIARD's "Teachers Must Learn."

Harlequin Romances . . . 6 exciting novels published each month! Each month you will get to know interesting, appealing, true-to-life people . . . . You'll be swept to distant lands you've dreamed of visiting . . . . Intrigue, adventure, romance, and the destiny of many lives will thrill you through each Harlequin Romance novel.

Get all the latest books before they're sold out!

As a Harlequin subscriber you actually receive your personal copies of the latest Romances immediately after they come off the press, so you're sure of getting all 6 each month.

Cancel your subscription whenever you wish!

You don't have to buy any minimum number of books. Whenever you decide to stop your subscription just let us know and we'll cancel all further shipments.

Your FREE gift includes

- **Anne Hampson** — Beyond the Sweet Waters
- **Anne Mather** — The Arrogant Duke
- **Violet Winspear** — Cap Flamingo
- **Nerina Hilliard** — Teachers Must Learn

FREE GIFT CERTIFICATE

and Subscription Reservation

Mail this coupon today!

In U.S.A.:
Harlequin Reader Service
MPO Box 707
Niagara Falls, NY 14302

In Canada:
Harlequin Reader Service
649 Ontario Street
Stratford, Ontario
N5A 6W4

Harlequin Reader Service:

Please send me my 4 Harlequin Romance novels
FREE. Also, reserve a subscription to the 6 NEW
Harlequin Romance novels published each month.
Each month I will receive 6 NEW Romance novels at
the low price of $1.25 each (Total — $7.50 a month).
There are no shipping and handling or any other
hidden charges. I may cancel this arrangement at any
time, but even if I do, these first 4 books are still mine
to keep.

_____

NAME   (PLEASE PRINT)

_____

ADDRESS

_____

CITY   STATE/PROV.   ZIP/POSTAL CODE

Offer not valid to present subscribers
Offer expires June 30, 1980   00356426100